© Brooke Guthrie

About the Author

LYDIA PEELLE was born in Boston. Her short stories have appeared in numerous publications and have won two Pushcart Prizes, an O. Henry Award, and been twice featured in *Best New American Voices*. She lives in Nashville, Tennessee.

Reasons for
and Advantages
of Breathing

Reasons for and Advantages of Breathing

Lydia Peelle

HARPER ● PERENNIAL

NEW YORK ● LONDON ● TORONTO ● SYDNEY ● NEW DELHI ● AUCKLAND

HARPER ● PERENNIAL

FIRST EDITION

Designed by Justin Dodd

Library of Congress Cataloging-in-Publication Data
Peelle, Lydia.
    Reasons for and advantages of breathing / Lydia Peelle. — 1st ed.
        p. cm.
    ISBN 978-0-06-172473-2
    1. Short stories, American. I. Title.
PS3616.E327R33 2009
813'.6—dc22   2008041939

09 10 11 12 13   OV/RRD   10 9 8 7 6 5 4 3 2

For Ketch

Acknowledgments

Grateful acknowledgment is made to the editors of the following publications, where these stories previously appeared in slightly different form: *Epoch*: "Mule Killers," which also appeared in *The O. Henry Prize Stories: 2006*; *Granta*: "Phantom Pain"; *The Sun*: "Sweethearts of the Rodeo," which also appeared in *Pushcart Prize XXXII*; *Epoch*: "The Still Point," which also appeared in *Best New American Voices* (2009); *One Story*: "Reasons for and Advantages of Breathing," which also appeared in *Pushcart Prize XXXIII*; *Orion*: "Kidding Season"; and *Prairie Schooner*: "Shadow on a Weary Land," which also appeared in *Best New American Voices* (2007).

Many thanks to the University of Virginia and the Fine Arts Work Center in Provincetown.

Contents

Reasons for
and Advantages
of Breathing

Mule Killers

My father was eighteen when the mule killers finally made it to his father's farm. He tells me that all across the state that year, big trucks loaded with mules rumbled steadily to the slaughterhouses. They drove over the roads that mules themselves had cut, the gravel and macadam that mules themselves had laid. Once or twice a day, he says, you would hear a high-pitched bray come from one of the trucks, a rattling as it went by, then silence, and you would look up from your work for a moment to listen to that silence. The mules when they were trucked away were sleek and fat on oats, work-shod and in their prime. *The best color is fat*, my grandfather used to say, when asked. But that year, my father tells me, that one heartbreaking year, the best color was dead. Pride and Jake and Willy Boy, Champ and Pete were dead, Kate and Sue and Orphan Lad, Orphan Lad was dead.

.   .   .

In the spring of that year, in the afternoon of a rain-brightened day, my father's father goes to Nashville and buys two International Harvester tractors for eighteen hundred dollars, cash. "We've got no choice nowadays," he tells the IHC man, counting out the bills and shaking his head. He has made every excuse not to buy a mule killer, but finally the farm's financial situation has made the decision for him. Big trucks deliver the tractors and unload them in the muddy yard in front of the barn, where for a day they hunch and sulk like children. My grandfather's tobacco fields stretch out behind them, shimmering in the spring heat. Beyond the slope of green, the Cumberland River is just visible through a fringe of trees, swollen and dark with rain.

The next morning, after chores, my grandfather calls in the hands to explain the basics of the new machines, just the way the man in Nashville has done for him. He stands next to one of the tractors for a long time, talking about the mechanics of it, one hand resting on its flank. Then with all the confidence he can muster he climbs up to start it. He tries three times before the tractor shivers violently, bucks forward, and busts the top rail of a fence. "This one ain't entirely broke yet," my grandfather jokes, struggling to back it up.

"Reckon you'll break it before it breaks you?" someone calls out, and only half of the men laugh. Most of them are used to sleeping all down the length of a tobacco row until the mules stop, waking just long enough to swing the team and start on back up the next. They all know when it's lunch-time because the mules bray, in unison, every day at five to twelve.

My father stands with the men who are laughing, laughing with them and scuffing up dust with his boot, though he is nervous about the tractors. His light eyes are squinted in the sun, and he slouches—he has his father's height, and he carries it apologetically. He is trying hard to keep certain things stuffed deep inside his chest: things like fear, sadness, and uncertainty. He expects to outgrow all of these things very soon, and in the meantime, he works hard to keep them hidden. Lately, he has become secretive about the things he loves. His love is fierce and full, but edged in guilt. He loves Orphan Lad: Orphan's sharp shoulders and soft ears, the mealy tuck of his lower lip. Music. Books and the smell of books, sun-warmed stones, and Eula Parker, who has hair thick and dark as soil. He has loved her since he was ten and once sat next to her at church; during the sermon she pinched him so hard his arm was red until Tuesday, and he had se-cretly kissed that red butterfly bruise. But Orphan will soon be gone, and none of the hands read books, and he laughs at the tractors just as he would laugh if one of these men made a rude comment about Eula Parker, because the most impor-tant thing, he believes, is not to let on that he loves anything at all.

Late that night, some of the hands sit on the porch to dip snuff and drink bitter cups of coffee. My father sits with them, silent on the steps. When he is with people he often finds pockets in the noise that he can crawl into and fill with his own thoughts, soft, familiar thoughts with worn, rounded corners. At this particular moment he is turning an old thought of Eula Parker over and over in his mind: he is going to marry her. If he goes so far as to conjure dark-haired children for them, I don't know, but he does build a house where they sit together on a porch, a vast and fertile farm on the other side of the river, and on this night, a shed full of bright chrome tractors, twice as big as the ones that rest still warm and ticking in his father's mule barn. He plants a flower garden for her at the foot of the porch; he buys a big Victrola for the dining room and a smaller, portable one for picnics. Guiltily he touches just the edges of one of these picnics: Eula's hair loose and wild, a warm blanket by a creek, cold chicken and hard-boiled eggs, drowsiness, possibility.

In a moment his pocket of quiet is turned inside out; the hands roar with laughter at the punch line of a joke and the screen door clatters as my grandfather comes out to the porch. "You all ever gonna sleep?" he asks them, and smiles. He is an old man, nearing seventy, and the thin length of his body has rounded to a stoop, like a sapling loaded with snow. But his eyes are still the eyes of a young man, even after years in the sun, and they are bright as he smiles and jokes. My father stands up and leans against a post, crossing his arms. His father winks at him, then waves his hand at the men and steps back into the house, shaking his head and chuckling.

·   ·   ·

My grandfather understood mule power. He celebrated it. He reveled in it. He always said that what makes a mule a better worker than the horse or the donkey is that he inherited the best from both of them: strong hindquarters from his dam and strong shoulders from his sire. He said, *The gospel according to mule is push and pull.* When his wife died young of a fever, it was not a horse but Orphan Lad who pulled her coffin slowly to the burying grounds, a thing the prouder men of the county later felt moved to comment on in the back room of the feed store. My grandfather was a man who never wore a hat, even to town. *Uncover thy head before the Lord,* he said, and the Lord he believed to be everywhere: in the trees, in the water of the creek, under Calumet cans rusting in the dirt.

Eula Parker is a slippery and mysterious girl, and my father's poor heart is constantly bewildered by her fickle ways. Like the day he walked her home from church and she allowed him to hold her cool hand, but would not let him see her all the way to the front door. Or the times when she catches him looking at her, and drops her eyes and laughs—at what, he cannot guess. With a kit he burns her name into a scrap of oak board and works up the courage to leave it at the door of her parents' house in town; when he walks by the next day and it is still there, he steals it back and takes it home to hide it shamefully beneath his bed. At church she always sits with the same girl, fifth pew back on the left, and he positions himself where he can see her: her hair swept up off her neck, thick purple-black and shining, the other girl's hanging limply down, onion-paper pale. Afterward, when people gather in the yard, the other girl always smiles at him, but he never notices; he is watching to see if Eula smiles, because sometimes she does and sometimes she doesn't. His love fattens on this until it is round and full, bursting from every seam.

At night, when he is sure his father is sleeping, he sticks the phonograph needle in a rubber eraser and holds the eraser in his front teeth. Carefully, with his nose inches from the record, he sets the needle down. With a hiss and crackle, the music reverberates through the hollows of his mouth and throat without making a sound in the room. Ignoring the cramp in his neck, this is how he listens to his favorite records night after night. Wild with thoughts of Eula with her hair like oil. Her snake-charming eyes. Her long, fine hands. How she teases him. He dreams he finds pieces of his heart in the boot scraper at her door.

On a warm and steamy afternoon my father makes a trip to town. He walks along the side of the road and passing cars do not give him any room. Several times he has to jump into the tick-heavy weeds that grow at the road's edge. At the river, a truck loaded with mules from a farm to the north passes him and bottoms out on the bridge. He keeps his head to the side until it is out of sight. Soon the truck will come for the last of his father's herd. *Oh, Orphan.* On the coldest mornings of his boyhood, his father had let him ride Orphan to school, bareback with two leads clipped to the halter. When they got to the schoolhouse he'd jump down and slap the mule's wide, wonderful haunch, and the big animal would turn without hesitation and walk directly home to be harnessed and hitched for the day's work.

Town is still and hot. The street is empty, buildings quiet, second-story shutters closed like eyes. He buys a tin of phonograph needles at the furniture store and lingers to look at the portable record players, nestled neat and tidy in their black cases. When he finally steps out of the store, head bowed in thought, he nearly runs into Eula and another girl, who stand bent close in serious conversation.

When they look up and see that it is him, they both politely say hello. Eula looks up at the store awning behind him. The other girl, the girl with the onion-pale hair, she looks down at the toe of her boot. He hears himself ask, "Want to go for a soda?" His voice is like a round stone that drops right there on the sidewalk. Eula's face closes like a door. But the other girl. The other girl, she guesses so.

He takes her to the only drugstore in town and they sit at the counter and order two sodas. She doesn't speak. They watch the clerk stocking packages on the high shelves along the wall, sliding his wooden ladder along the track in the ceiling with a satisfying, heavy sound. She seals her straw with her finger and swizzles it around the glass. She crosses her right ankle over her left, then her left ankle over her right, then hooks her heels onto the bottom of the stool. My father compliments her on her dress. The clerk drops a bag of flour and curses, then apologizes to the girl. There are hollow fly carcasses wedged into the dusty seam of the counter and the warped wood floor. Even with two ceiling fans running, the air is hot and close.

This must have been the middle of August; though my father doesn't tell me this, it is easy enough to count backwards and figure for myself. The walls of the store are painted a deep green and the paint has bubbled in some places. My father's mind fails him as he searches for something to say. He watches her twist a strand of hair around her finger, but she feels his eyes on her and abruptly stops, folding her hands in her lap.

"So, you and Eula, y'all sit together at church," he says, forgetting to make it a question.

Puzzled, the girl nods her head. She has not yet said a word. Perhaps she is having trouble believing that she is sitting here at this counter, having a soda with a boy. Or she is worrying that her hair is too pale and limp, or her wrists too big, or her dress too common. She has never believed she would find herself in this situation, and so has never rehearsed.

"I've always thought this time of year is the saddest," she finally says, looking up at my father. He lays his hand on the counter and spreads out his fingers. His chin tilts forward as if he is about to speak. Then the sleigh bells on the door jingle, shiver when it slams shut. It is Eula. She doesn't look at them. She brushes her sweat-damp hair back with two fingers and asks the clerk for something—what?—my father's ears are suddenly filled—she is asking the clerk for a tin of aspirin, peering up at the shelves behind him and blinking those eyes. The clerk stares too long before turning to his ladder. My father considers socking him one in that plug-ugly face. Eula raps her fingers along the edge of the counter and hums tunelessly, and still she won't look their way.

At this moment, my father feels his heart dissolve into a sticky bright liquid. Jealousy has seized her, she has followed them here—he is certain. Finally, a staggering proclamation of her love. His heart has begun to trickle down into the soles of his feet when the girl somehow catches Eula's eye and ripples her fingers at her.

Hello.

Then Eula unfolds her long body towards them, and smiles. An enormous, beautiful, open-faced smile: a smile with no jealousy hidden behind it at all. She takes her change and paper sack from the clerk and turns, one hand stretched out towards the door. She is simply going to leave. She is going to walk out the door and leave them here to their sodas and silence. At this point my father, frantic, takes hold of the girl on the stool next to him, leans her in Eula's direction, and kisses her recklessly, right on the mouth.

My father tells me this story in the garden, bent over and searching through the knee-high weeds for long, thick stalks of asparagus, clipping them with his pocket knife and handing them to me. Here he stops and straightens and squints east, and I know his back is starting to bother him. Why he never told me the story when I was a boy, I don't know; I am twice as old now as he was, the year of the mule killers. But still he skips the part of the story where I come in.

It doesn't matter; I can imagine it. Before the door has even closed after Eula, something has changed in my father, and as he slides from his stool he firmly takes the girl's hand. He leads her out of the drugstore, glancing back once more at the pock-faced clerk, who is carefully smoothing Eula's dollar bill into the cash register drawer. Slowly they make their way somewhere: back to the farm, most likely, where his father is sitting with the hands at supper. He takes her to the hayloft, a back field, the mule barn, the spring house: anyplace that was dark and quiet for long enough that my father could desperately try to summon Eula's face, or else hope to forever blot it from his mind. Long enough that I, like a flashbulb, could snap into existence.

"Mercy, mercy, mercy," my grandfather said, that day they finally took Orphan. "He'll be all right." He pinched the bridge of his nose and looked away when they tried to load Orphan onto the truck. The mule's big ears swung forward, his narrow withers locked, and he would not budge when he got to the loading ramp. It took four men to finally get him up, and they saw his white eye swiveling madly when they looked in through the slats. "Not stubborn, just smart," my grandfather said to the ground, then again pinched his nose and leaned against the truck as two more mules were loaded up. His herd was so big that this was the last of three trips. He had intended to send Orphan with the first load, but had put it off and put it off.

"Ain't it some kind of thanks," my grandfather said as he latched up the back of the truck, the mules inside jostling to get their footing, and Orphan's long ear had swiveled back at the sound of his voice. The best of them brought three or four cents a pound as dog meat; some of them would merely be heaved six deep into a trench that would be filled in with dirt by men on tractors. The hollow report of hooves on the truck bed echoed even after the truck had pulled onto the road and turned out of sight. The exact same sound could be heard all through the county, all across the hills of Tennessee and up through Kentucky, across Missouri and Kansas, and all the way out West, even, you could hear it. The mules' job, it was finished.

When the back of the truck is finally shut, my father is high above, hiding in the hayloft. At church the pale-haired girl had pulled him into the center aisle just before the service and told him her news, the news of me. All through the sermon his mind had flipped like a fish, and he had stared hard at the back of Eula's neck, trying to still that fish. In the hayloft he thinks of this moment as he listens to the shouts of the truck driver and the engine backfiring once before the mules are pulled away, but he doesn't come to the edge, he doesn't look down for one last glimpse of Orphan Lad.

Late that night my father creeps to the Victrola in the living room and carefully opens the top of the cabinet. He slides a record onto the turntable and turns the crank, then sets his eraser and needle between his teeth and presses it to the first groove. A fiddle plays, is joined by a guitar, and then a high lonesome voice starts in about heartbreak. Every time he listens to his records like this, the first notes take him by surprise. When the music starts to fill his head, he can't believe it is coming from the record on the turntable and not from a place within himself. He closes his eyes and imagines Eula Parker is in the room, dancing behind him in a dark red dress. He moves his face across the record, following the groove with the needle, and spit collects in the pockets of his cheeks. *Eula, Eula, Eula.* He lets her name roll around in his head until it is unclear, too, whether this sound is coming from the record on the turntable, or from the deepest hollows of his heart.

Three weeks after the last load of mules goes, a tractor overturns on a hill down by the river and nearly kills one of the hands. It is not an unexpected tragedy. My grandfather is the only one with the man, and he pulls him out from underneath the seat and searches through the grass for three scattered fingers while the engine continues to choke and whir. He drives the man to the hospital in Nashville and doesn't return until late that night. His trip home is held up by an accident at the bridge that takes nearly an hour to be cleared away. When he finally arrives back, his son is waiting on the porch to tell him about the pale-haired girl.

My father has rehearsed what he will say dozens of times to the fence posts and icebox, but when he sees his father's brown, blood-caked forearms and hands, he is startled enough to forget what it was. Weary and white in the face, my grandfather sits down next to him on the top step and touches his shoulder.

"Son," he says, "you're gonna see a future I can't even stretch my mind around. Not any of it. I can't even begin to imagine."

If my father had understood what his father was trying to tell him, maybe he would have waited until the morning to say what he now says. Maybe he would never had said anything, packed up a small bag, and left town for good. Abandoned love and any expectation of it. Instead he confesses to my grandfather, all in a rush, the same way he might have admitted that he had broken the new mower, or left the front gate open all night.

My grandfather stares hard at my father's knee and is quiet a long time.

"You done her wrong," he says. Repeats it. "You got no choice but to take care of it. You done her wrong."

In those days this was my grandfather's interpretation of the world: A thing was either right or it was wrong. Or so it seemed to my father, and he was getting tired of it.

"No, sir," he says, lips tight. "That's not what I intend. I'm in love with someone else." He takes a breath. "I'm gonna

marry Eula Parker." Even as he speaks her name he is star-
tled by this statement, like it is a giant carp he has yanked
from the depths of the river. It lies on the step before both of
them, gasping.

My grandfather looks at him with sadness rimming his eyes
and says quietly, "You should've thought of that before."

"But you see," my father says, as if explaining to a child,
"I love her."

My grandfather grips his knees with his big hands and sighs.
He reaches out for his son's arm, but my father brushes him
away, stands up, and walks heavily across the porch. When he
goes into the house, he lets the screen door slam behind him,
and it bangs twice in the casement before clicking shut.

Late that night, after washing the dishes of a silent dinner,
my father sits on the porch sharpening his pocket knife. He
taps his bare feet against the hollow stairs and even whistles
through his teeth. His father's words have still not completely
closed in around him. Though an uneasiness is slowly creep-
ing up, he is still certain that the future is bright chrome and
glorious, full of possibility. Behind him, a string of the banjo
gently twangs as it goes flat in the cooling air. It is the first
night of the year that smells of autumn and my father takes
a few deep breaths as he leans against the porch railing and
looks out into the yard. This is when he sees something out
under the old elm, a long, twisted shape leaning unsteadily
against the thick trunk of the tree.

He steps off the porch onto the cool grass of the yard, thinking first he sees a ghost. As he gets closer to the shape, he believes it next to be a fallen limb, or one of the hands, drunk on moonshine—then, nothing but a forgotten ladder, then—with rising heart—Eula come to call for him in her darkest dress. But when he is just a few yards away from the tree, he sees it is his father, his back to the house, arms at his sides. He is speaking quietly, and my father knows by the quality of his voice that he is praying. He has found him like this before, in the hayfield at dusk or by the creek in the morning, eyes closed, mumbling simple private incantations. My father is about to step quietly back to the porch when his father reaches a trembling hand to the tree to steady himself, then lets his shoulders collapse. He blows his nose in his hand and my father hears him swallow back thick, jumbled sobs. When he hears this, when he realizes his father is crying, he turns and rushes blindly back to the house, waves of heat rising from beneath his ribs like startled birds from a tree.

Once behind the closed door of his room, my father makes himself small as possible on the edge of his unmade bed. Staring hard at the baseboard, he tries to slow his tumbling heart. He has never seen his father cry, not even when his mother died. Now, having witnessed it, he feels like he has pulled the rug of manhood out from under the old man's feet. He convinces himself that it must be the lost mules his father was praying for, or for the mangled man who lies unconscious in the hospital bed in Nashville, and that this is what drove him to tears. It is only much later, picking asparagus in the ghost of a garden, that he will admit who his father had really been crying for: for his son, and for *his* son.

These days, my father remembers little from the time before the tractors. The growl of their engines in his mind has long since drowned out the quieter noises: the constant stamping and shifting of mule weight in the barn, the smooth sound of oats being poured into a steel bucket. He remembers the steam that rose from the animals after work. Pooled heaps of soft leather harness waiting to be mended on the breakfast table. At the threshold of the barn door, a velvet-eared dog that was always snapping its teeth at flies. Orphan standing dark and noble in the snow, a sled hooked to his harness. Eula Parker in a dark blue hat laughing and saying his name, hurrying after him and calling out "Wait, wait," one warm Sunday as he left church for home.

He remembers too his mother's cooking spices lined up in the cupboard where they had been since her death, faded inside their tins, without scent or taste. When he knew he was alone in the house, it gave him some sad comfort to take them out one by one and open them, the contents of each as dusty and gray as the next. He has just one memory of her, just an image: the curve of her spine and the fall of her hair when she had once leaned over to sniff the sheets on his bed, the morning after he'd wet it. This is all he has of her: one moment, just one, tangled in those little threads of shame.

In the same way I only have one memory of my grandfather, one watery picture from when I was very young. When my mother and father would rock me on the porch at night, my grandfather sat with them in a straight-backed chair, playing the banjo. He would tie a little tissue paper doll to his right wrist, and it danced and jumped like a tiny white ghost. I remember sitting on my mother's lap one night, and in the darkness the only things I could see were the tissue doll, the white moon of the banjo face, my mother's pale hair. I remember watching that doll bobbing along with my grandfather's strumming and, from time to time, the white flash of his teeth when he smiled. And I can hear him sing just a piece of one of the old songs: *I know'd it, indeed I know'd it, yes, I know'd it, my bones are gonna rise again.*

This is the story that my father tells me as he bends like a wire wicket in the garden, or, I should say, what once was my mother's garden. He parts the tangle of weeds to find the asparagus, then snaps off the tough spears with his knife, straightening slowly from time to time to stretch his stiff and rounded back. The garden is like a straight-edged wilderness in the middle of the closely mowed lawn, a blasted plot of weeds and thorns and thistle. Nothing has grown here since my mother died and no one wanted to tend it. Nothing except the asparagus, which comes up year after year.

Phantom Pain

Something's out there. Something has shown up in the woods of Highland City. Dave Hardy was the first to see it, the opening weekend of bow season, up in his grandfather's tree stand on the hill behind Walmart. Afterwards he bushwhacked hell-bent down to the parking lot, and, gasping for breath, tried to tell the story to anyone who would listen. The story changed with the telling, and after a while, Dave Hardy himself didn't know what to believe: *See that old pine tree over there? It was close to me as that tree. As close as that blue Honda over there. As close as you to me.*

Panther. Painter. Puma. Cougar. Mountain lion. Whatever you want to call it, by the end of October, half a dozen more people claim they have caught a glimpse of it: a pale shiver in the distance, a flash of fur through the trees. In the woods, hunters linger in their tree stands, hoping they might be the next. In the houses, the big cat creeps nightly, making the rounds of dinner tables and dreams.

Twenty years in a taxidermy shop and Jack Wells has heard his share of tall tales, near misses, the one that got away. But the panther stories are different, told with pitch and fervor, a wild look in the eye. They don't carry much truck with Jack. No one, after all, has any sort of proof—a photo, a positively identifiable set of tracks, or even a really good look at the thing. For all Jack is concerned, it's an overgrown coyote, someone's German shepherd, or a figment of everyone's imagination. A mountain lion in Highland City? Sure, there's woods out there, hills with deep hollers and abandoned tobacco fields; not a whole lot of people, nothing to the south but the PLAXCO plant, nothing to the north but Kentucky—but the chances are just as good you'll run into a woolly mammoth. People, if you ask Jack, have lost all sense.

His ex-wife Jeanne is the worst of them, jabbering on about it like it's some kind of cuddly pussy cat.

"Oh, isn't it something!" she tells Jack, when they bump into one another in the frozen foods aisle of Tony's Shur-Save. "Wouldn't I like to catch me a glimpse of it."

Jack is on one of the store's motorized scooters, the basket filled with items he has begrudgingly picked from the doctor's new list: brown rice, cottage cheese, egg replacer. He is embarrassed by the scooter, and when he realizes Jeanne isn't going to say anything about it he feels worse, and he shifts around on the seat, boxed in by his shame.

"For Christ's sake, Jeanne. There's nothing out there."

Jeanne lets go of her cart and puts her hands on her hips, cocks her head at him, and gives him a look. "And how do *you* know?"

"Because I seen everything that come out of these woods the last twenty years. Every buck, doe, weasel, turkey, tick, and flea. There ain't no panther out there. There ain't been a panther for over ninety years."

"Well," Jeanne says, pursing her lips, considering this. "There is now."

At the end of the summer, seven weeks ago, Jack lost his left leg below the knee, the latest battleground of his diabetes. He has only just returned to work full-time, and the walk-in freezer is stuffed with back orders: stiff red foxes stacked six deep and more buck head-and-shoulders than Jack cares to shake a stick at. Finished work crowds the shop: dozens of bucks, turkeys, coons, squirrels on cured oak branches, largemouth bass on maple plaques, all waiting to be picked up by customers.

Ronnie, the latest in a long line of apprentices, still around only because he hasn't knocked up a girl or blown his face up cooking meth, sits just outside the walk-in in a ski parka, defrosting a mink skin with a hair dryer and grunting along to the radio. He came in three days a week and did prep work while Jack was recovering, leaving a pile of buck capes so sloppily fleshed out that Jack has to go back over each one of them with a razor blade to get rid of the leftover bits of fat and vein. Jack is sitting at his workbench, shaking out a cramp in his hand and cursing the day Ronnie was born, when Jeanne comes in, the bell on the door jingling.

"Well, well, well," Jack says to the full-body doe mount that stands next to him, ears pricked, front hoof raised, frozen in the moment just before flight. "Don't look now."

For twenty years, since Jack started the taxidermy business, Jeanne has come down to the shop from the house at least twice a day: in the morning to bring the sorted mail and in the evening to do the receipts and sweep. Four days a week, she works down at the elementary school in the principal's office, a job she's had for forty years, since the summer after they got married. Jeanne kept the house in the divorce. Jack moved into a little trailer on what was left of his father's tobacco holdings, where he's been ever since. But his shop remained in their old two-car garage, a hundred yards down the hill from the house. It's a good spot—tucked up against a wooded hill, no neighbors for miles. He would never be able to rent a place like this, and even back then the shop had become something of an institution among the men of Highland City. The thing he didn't anticipate was that the thin path that links the house to the shop would persist, worn down to the hard dirt through the years by his steps, now by Jeanne's. Jeanne does the ordering, the taxes, the books. Ask Jack Wells how his ex-wife is and he'll shrug and roll his eyes and always give the same answer: *Around*.

"All right, Hud, shoe off!" Jeanne claps her hands with cheerful authority. Once a week, for the six weeks he's been

home since the surgery, she has insisted on cutting the toe-
nails of Jack's good foot. This was how it started, on the other
side: an ingrown toenail, a raging infection, his circulation
shot to hell from the diabetes. Jeanne driving white-knuckled
to the emergency room.

Jack throws down the buck cape and pushes his stool back
with a screech. "Where's the dog?"

He peers into the open doorway behind her. Tiny, Jeanne's
ancient and devoted black-and-tan beagle, was banished last
week after lifting his leg on a turkey.

"In the house. Don't you worry about him. I told him, I
said, 'Tiny, I'm not letting you out of my sight anymore, you
hear me?'" She raises her voice an octave, to the singsong
tone she uses with the dog. "No, sir. Not with that mean old
hungry panther prowling around here. Uh-uh. Not out of my
sight."

She takes off her windbreaker and lays it carefully be-
tween two raccoons, nostrils stuffed with cotton batting, that
are drying on the plywood table in the middle of the room.
"Now. I want to get this over with just as much as you do,
Huddie, so be a good boy and give me something for under
my knees. These old bones can't take no more kneeling on
concrete floors."

As she struggles to her knees on his corduroy jacket, he
looks down at her. The top of her head is so familiar. The
same perm she has always worn, only gray now instead of
red-brown: a black-and-white photo of her younger self. He
feels a startling rise of anticipation for her warm, wet mouth,

a forty-year-old memory stirred by the sight of her head at his lap: the two of them in the backseat of his car at the drive-in. But then she pulls the little leather kit out of her pocket and unfolds it to reveal an array of cold, sharp metal tools, and he coughs and shifts his weight, embarrassed, as if she can read his mind.

"Let's get this over with," he barks.

Jeanne furrows her brow in concentration as she sets to work on each tough yellow nail. Jack folds his arms across his chest and puffs out his cheeks, letting out a long breath. His stomach is bothering him. His stomach is always bothering him. It gurgles and spits, clenches and churns. The pills do it to him. The doctor gave him another set of prescriptions after this latest round in the hospital, after he made it through the unbearable days of physical therapy. He frowns and studies his gut, like a basketball under his shirt. He can't see beyond it to his foot, or to the metal rods of his prosthesis that peek out under his left cuff. In six weeks he goes back for the permanent one, the one that is supposed to be so lifelike he will forget it's not his.

"Betty Ann Flowers called last night. Her new miniature schnauzer? Missing. Disappeared clear out of her yard. That dog cost her four hundred dollars, too." Jeanne draws in her breath. "Can you even imagine? I told Tiny, I said, 'Not out of my—'"

"Careful," Jack snaps.

"I *am* being careful, Huddie." Jeanne sighs. She can't understand why he doesn't see that this is all for his own good. He seems to think she *wants* to do this. She shoots him a look. His face, between the jowls, is the same as it has always been, like a familiar road widened for shoulders. She wonders if he is really watching his weight. He seems heavier. Her breath catches in her throat, and she looks back down quickly, scolding herself for worrying. In high school, she'd thought he looked like—just a little bit like—Paul Newman. Not the eyes—Jack's were brown and sleepy—but in the chin, mostly. They saw *Hud* down at the drive-in when they were first married, and she teasingly nicknamed him after the movie's cold-hearted, cheating hero. By the time the bad years rolled around, they were both so used to the name that neither one drew the connection to see the irony.

CAT FEVER, reads the headline of the *Highland City Gazette* on the first day of rifle season. There are two pictures below: a stock photograph of a mountain lion, teeth bared, ears pinned back, and a grainy photograph of Dave Hardy with another man Jack doesn't recognize, serious looks set on their faces, crouched next to a wash somewhere up in the woods. An inset shows what they are pointing to: a blurred set of tracks in the mud, which mysteriously disappear, according to the caption, after only a few feet.

"Could have been made by anything," Jack tells Ronnie, peering down his nose at the paper. "Coyote. Bobcat. Some little old *dog*. Listen. We just don't have the wilderness to hold an animal of that size. Scraggly third-growth hardwoods chopped up by logging roads and so full of hunters on ATVs it's a wonder they don't shoot each others' nuts off. A panther, first of all, is secretive and shy. Second, they can cover some ground. Fifteen, twenty miles a day. There just isn't the room. He'd keep bumping up against highways."

"It's hogwash," Jack tells Jeanne later, when she's down in the afternoon to sweep. The pain in his stump has been building all day, like a swarm of ants. He wants to go home and lie down in the dark and not have to see or talk to anyone for days. "Where would it have come from in the first place? Closest it might have wandered in from, closest those things live to us is the wildest bayous of Louisiana. You mean to tell me that a hundred-fifty-pound cat wandered out of some canebrake jungle, walked seven hundred miles without being sighted once, crossed four-lane roads and subdivisions and schoolyards, and took up residence here? In *Highland City*?"

"Well," Jeanne says quietly, "you don't have to *yell*. And who knows? Maybe it didn't walk. Maybe it climbed up and fell asleep in a boxcar somewhere. Maybe it came on a *train*."

Late on a Friday afternoon, Jack stops Ronnie as he's leaving the shop and asks if he's given any thought to his future. "I'm not going to be at this forever, you know," Jack tells him. "If you put a little more into it, you could be taking over here in a couple of years." But Ronnie doesn't think much about his future at all, at least not the kind measured in years. Ronnie has been thinking, lately, about quite a few other things: If he has enough credit to put a down payment on an ATV. If mountain lions are attracted to catnip. If he should ask his girlfriend, Tanya, to move in with him. Tanya is nineteen and a poet. Later that night, he picks her up at work and they drink a pitcher of beer up at Sullivan's. She sits across from him in their booth and scrawls in a big loose-leaf notebook while he watches a wrestling match on the TV above the bar. His sweatshirt and glasses are flecked with blood and bits of fatty tissue. Jack is always trying to get him to change his clothes when he leaves work. "You can't be taking a girl on a date dressed like that!" But Tanya doesn't care, or at least has never said anything.

"You know what I wanna do?" he says, eyes on the screen. "Get me one of them flat-screen TVs. One of them big ones."

Tanya looks up at him, her pen in her mouth, and doesn't say a word. She is writing a poem about the panther. All her life, one thing has been sure: nothing ever happens in Highland City. Now this. She believes it is some sort of sign.

The feet contain a quarter of all the bones in the human body, the doctors told Jack when he was in the hospital. Well, Jack asked, how many bones are in the human body, anyway? Depending on how you count the sternum bones, 206 or 208. So: the bones of one foot, plus one leg from the knee down—count them—he was what, one-eighth gone? He thinks about this often—too often. In bed, trying to sleep, he stuffs a pillow over the place where his left leg should be, the way the nurses showed him. When that does nothing to calm the pain, he lurches out of bed and finds the heaviest book in the house. When that doesn't work, he flings it across the room, pounds the mattress, and bites the pillow. His leg. Sometimes he has a panicky thought that they gave it to Jeanne, in a jar, like a tonsil. And that she has it up there in the house, with all his things: his old records and taxidermy videos, the suit he wore at their wedding, his .22, and his mother's Bible. All those other things he would have said twenty years ago were essential but had proven after all not to be.

Ray Blevins finds a dead fawn under his tree stand, all ripped to hell, half-buried in the leaves like something is planning to return for it. He comes up to the shop for no other reason than to tell this story to Jack. Ray is one that Jack has a hard time finding any respect for. One of the big talkers who needs a dozen technological gadgets to bring down a measly spike buck, who wants to go out there on a Saturday morning with his cell phone and his GPS system, his digital estrus bleat caller and human scent killer and eight-hundred-dollar rifle, and pretend he is Daniel Boone, out on the knife-edge of danger, deep in the uncharted wilderness. But a man couldn't get lost out there if he tried. That's why Jack quit hunting long ago, even before he got sick—because you simply can't get lost anymore—and where's the excitement and danger and pleasure in that? Even if your GPS broke and your cell phone fell in the mud, if you didn't run into another yahoo doing the same thing ten yards down the hill then you could just follow the sound of the highway, find the gas station, and call your wife.

"You know," Ray says, jabbing his finger at the window. "They say one of these cats will follow you. Read about a man out in Colorado got followed for *twenty* miles. They're just curious, though. Worst thing you can do is run. You run, well, then, kiss it good-bye. Get your jugular torn right out. If you know one's behind you, you just got to keep your cool, keep going on about your business."

Jack gives the clock a good long look, but Ray keeps going.

"Ten feet. Ten feet, they can pounce from a standstill. Tell that to your kid on his walk to school in the morning. Tell that to these people who think we should let this thing be."

"Tell that to my ex-wife, then," Jack says, turning away. "She seems to think we should put a cozy little wicker basket and a scratching post out for it."

Ray snorts. "People just don't understand. What we have here, what we've got on our hands is a *monster.*"

Those who have heard it say the call of a mountain lion is like the scream of a woman, more chilling, more hopeless, than anything you will hear in your life. The scream of a woman whose child has been wrenched from her arms and who is now watching, helplessly, as the last breath is choked out of it.

The fact that no one in Highland City has heard such a night-ripping scream is one of the many points that Jack constantly brings up in support of finding another explanation. What he does not tell anyone, not even Jeanne, is the sound that he himself heard one night, a week ago, at the moment he found a way to creep around the pain and part the curtains of a dream. Suddenly he was wide awake, heart pounding, terrified, thinking, *What was that? What the hell was that?*

But what with the painkillers he was still on. And the awful nights' sleep he's been having. Of course there's an explanation. It was nothing more than a terrible hallucination. And yet for the past week he has kept the television on all night, the volume turned up loud. Just for company.

Kenny Peabody buys a number 4½ steel bear trap with a double-pronged drag hook on an eight-foot chain and hauls a dead calf for bait up the hillside behind the filling station and when word gets out about it, all hell breaks loose. "We need to take action," men start saying. "For the safety of our women and children. Before something happens that we all regret." Some Rotarians get together and invest in night-vision goggles and go out every midnight with an arsenal and don't come home until sunrise. Jack shakes his head and wonders how soon before someone gets himself shot. Whatever that thing might turn out to be, he thinks, why not just leave it the hell in peace? Every third customer who comes in asks if Jack will mount the cat for him if he bags it. And Jack, weary, counters with the oldest joke in the book: "Sure, Bud. Two for one and we'll do your ex-wife too."

They slap him on the back, sending a tide of pain down his spine. "Good one, Jack!" they all say.

One morning Ronnie grabs a pencil from Jack's workbench, draws something on the back of an envelope, and thrusts it in front of Jack. He's breathing through his nose, his glasses slipped down, his flabby face trembling. "I seen it," he says. "Out on the road last night. I seen it! Scared the shit out of me. Nearly wrecked."

Jack squints at the picture: a primitive cave painting, a child's crayon drawing. "You saw a water buffalo?"

Ronnie stares at him. He hits the paper with the end of the pencil. "The *cougar*. Last night, around eleven. I was leaving Sullivan's. I caught it in my high beams, coming around that bend. It was there on the shoulder. Then it just disappeared into the trees. I pulled over but it was long gone."

"You don't say."

Jack considers the drawing again. It reminds him of the first couple of mounts Ronnie has attempted himself, a coon and a pintail duck: graceless, stiff, hastily and sloppily done. You have to lose yourself in the work, Jack has always believed. At some point in the process, even for a few minutes—and it sounds like a bunch of hocus-pocus—you have to let the animal lead you. After all, it's not clay or paint or iron you're working with. What you're working with has, up until recently, been a living, breathing thing, for years has been blinking, snorting, sleeping, grazing, scanning the horizon.

You have to respect that. You have to get in touch with that, if you want to come close to reproducing it.

"Believe it now?" Ronnie says, striking the paper with the pencil.

"I'll believe it when I see it," Jack says, feeling suddenly depressed. He's ready to go home, lie down on the couch, turn the television on, fry up a pork chop. To hell with his new diet.

"That bitch is mine," Ronnie says, as if Jack has suggested otherwise. "That son of a bitch is *all mine.*"

Up on the ridge under Ray Blevins's tree stand, the dead fawn's flesh is stripped away by coyote, then fox, then possum, their eyes glinting as they visit it in the night, tiny teeth tearing. The ants come too. Whatever killed it does not come back. Soon all that is left is the rib cage, looming on the hilltop like an empty basket.

One chilly December afternoon, the smell of snow in the air, Tanya comes to the shop to pick up Ronnie, whose truck isn't running again. Pulling up the drive, she sees Jeanne in the yard, fussing around with her birdfeeders, squat and round in her big down parka, her glasses on a string around her neck. What is it with old people and birds? Tanya wonders. She thinks of her grandmother, the device she has with the microphone outside so she can sit in her living room and listen to the birds while she watches her soaps on television. If I ever end up like that, she thinks, climbing out of the car and skirting a puddle in the driveway. Stuck rotting away inside while the world goes on outside. Well, somebody just *shoot* me.

When Tanya comes in, Ronnie is working outside the walk-in with a buck head that is hanging upside down on a heavy chain. He is slowly pulling off the cape from the shoulders forward, until it hangs inside out, dangling from the end of the nose like a sock. Exposed is the gleaming naked head, white subcutaneous fat, dark veins, lidless, staring eyes. Jack started the fleshing-out himself but didn't get past struggling with the winch. Now he's sitting at his workbench, hands on his knees, trying to catch his breath. He watches Tanya go straight over to Ronnie and lay into him, their voices sharp across the shop. Jack is impressed by how she doesn't take a second look at the buck—even Jeanne, after all these years, can't go near them when they're at this stage. After a few minutes she turns her back on Ronnie and, looking over at Jack, raises her hand to wave. He waves back. To his surprise, she comes over.

"Hey," she says, almost flirtatious. "Want to see my new tattoo?"

Before he can answer, she yanks the neck of her sweatshirt off her shoulder and turns around. On her shoulder blade, there are four short slash marks and a drop of ruby blood. At first Jack thinks it is a real wound. She lowers her voice and steals a glance at Ronnie, then levels her gaze at Jack.

"Ronnie thinks it's all a load of bull, but that panther is

my totem animal. Want to know how I know? It came to me in a dream and told me so."

Jack wishes there was some way to hide his heaving gut. He points to the tattoo. "You're going to have that the rest of your life."

"Well, *yeah*."

He's got one himself, from his stint in the army—a cloverleaf on his bicep, with his infantry division printed inside; they all got the same one, one night in Texas. All the color is faded out now except the blue. What he really means to say—how can he explain it? The rest of your life, Tanya, is a hell of a lot longer than you think it will be. And you'll grow tired of everything. Your own face in the mirror. The sound of your own voice. And that's when you'll start regretting that tattoo. Not because you see it every day. But because you don't even notice it anymore. Because you thought it *would* last forever, and remind you of something forever. And it doesn't.

On December 15, at one-thirty in the afternoon, Jack drives to the medical center in Scottsville to be fitted with his permanent limb. He has rescheduled the appointment once already, dreading it, moaning about it for a week until Jeanne finally said, "Oh, Hud! Grow up and just go!"

The nurse takes his blood pressure and vital signs as impersonally as if she were trussing a turkey. When she asks how he is feeling, he catches her eye and smiles, trying to flirt a little.

"Well, what can I say? I've got one foot in the grave."

She gives him a blank look and a feeble, false smile that makes him feel old and ridiculous in his flimsy gown. Then she goes out into the hall and returns with his new limb. It is eerily lifelike, down to the wrinkles on the toes, and the exact same color as his flesh. "You'll forget it's not yours," she says brightly, as she shows him how to put it on. "And it's flame-resistant."

Jack scrolls through the possibilities for a wisecrack, but finds he simply does not have the energy. "Fine," he finally says. "Good."

The doctor is in and out in three minutes, barely raising his eyes from Jack's chart. "Any questions?" he says as he goes, not leaving room for a yes. He is already tucking his pen in his breast pocket, checking his watch, and groping for the door handle behind him.

Jack is suddenly alone, left sitting on the table with a pamphlet in his hand: LIFE WITH YOUR NEW LIMB. It is filled with glossy photos of retirees acting like giddy teenagers: walking hand in hand on the beach, bowling, ballroom dancing—the woman with a rose clamped between her dentures. *Don't ever admit anything has changed,* they're screaming at him. *Never for a minute slow down or feel sorry for yourself. Look at us!* He crumples the pamphlet and throws it in the trash can.

I do have a question, Doc, he thinks, sitting there, his shoulders hunched. Actually, I do. What the hell am I supposed to do now? There is something he hasn't had the nerve to tell anyone yet: he doesn't think he can go on with his work. He has never before realized how physical it is:

the lifting, the sawing, six or seven solid hours on his feet—foot—a day. And it's not just the stump, the gone leg. He's exhausted to the core. Just yesterday he had to ask Ronnie to finish a coon for him—a simple little raccoon—he got so winded, trying to stretch the cape around the form. Somebody tell me what to do, he thinks, struggling to pull his pants on over the new limb, disgusted by it as if it's a bad joke, a gag trick. Somebody tell me just exactly what it is I'm supposed to do now.

On the way back to Highland City, Jack takes the old road instead of the highway, the pike that stretches all the way up to Kentucky. It follows the natural valley of the hills and was the route the long hunters followed, two hundred years ago, when they came to these woods from the north to harvest the buffalo and deer. Jack's father used to tell him stories of the long hunters. They'd arrive with nothing but a gun and an ax, build a log cabin and stay for a year, eating deer meat and salting the skins, which they rolled up on a travois and brought home when they simply couldn't carry any more. Parklike forests, great open spaces under magnificently canopied trees. When the first of them came down from Kentucky, his father told him, they did not dismount, lest they be trampled, the woods were so crowded with game.

Jack tries to picture it, squinting up into the sparse trees on the hillside along the pike, but he can't. It must have been something like being in the shop, he decides. Big-antlered deer standing shoulder to shoulder, fox and weasels cheek to jowl. Except also wolf and bear. Mountain lion.

What if? Jack thinks, entering the Highland City limits. What if there really *is* a mountain lion up there? The houses huddle on either side of the pike, brick and squat, with carports and dog runs, the older ones at the edges of the last few tobacco fields, the farmers inside in front of their TVs, getting paid by Uncle Sam not to grow tobacco. He passes the gas stations, the cinderblock barbeque stand, the shopping center, the new shopping center. The smokestacks of the PLAXCO plant poke up out of the hills to the south, crowned by white smoke.

If a panther really *is* up there, sniffing out an ancient path its great-great ancestors once followed, is at this very moment twitching its great muscular tail and arching its back to run its claws down the trunk of a tree, dropping to all fours to nose at a beef jerky wrapper filled with dirty rainwater and picking around rusted old tin cans and television sets to make its way into one of those hollers, meowing a lonely meow, well—Jack thinks, pulling in his driveway and stopping to check the empty mailbox in front of his trailer—then I *pity* the old bastard.

Tanya, alone in Ronnie's house, takes off all her clothes and lies down on the couch, staring at the blank space on the wall, cleared of posters to make room for his new TV. She's been driving back and forth to her place all day, bringing the last of her stuff over. Now she wishes it would all disappear. All those things that seemed so special when she bought them: her leather jacket, her laptop, her world map shower curtain, her black boots, it all looks like a load of junk, now, stacked up in liquor boxes on Ronnie's kitchen floor. Moving in with Ronnie is the start of something, she knows, but she also knows that it is maybe not the start she was looking for. She closes her eyes and pictures herself hovering above all of her possessions, flying away. She imagines herself in a forest. A dark, deep forest. Walking out into it, naked, and never coming back. She hears Ronnie fumble with his keys at the front door, swearing. She disappears into a cathedral of trees.

Tiny goes missing. Jeanne calls Jack late on a Sunday to tell him, apologizes if she's interrupting anything. He has been watching a tedious sitcom, his prosthesis off, the stump tucked away out of sight under a blanket. The bowl of chili he spilled reaching for the phone is splattered all over the floor. He looks at it dolefully. Well, it was giving him heartburn, and he shouldn't be eating that junk, anyway. He pounds his chest and burps.

"Now, Huddie, I don't want to jump to no conclusions. But that cat, Hud—it could have just come down out of the woods behind the house and waited. I let him out for five minutes. *Five minutes.* That panther could have just slunk in and—oh! I've got goose pimples just thinking about it—carried him away."

Jack can picture her perfectly, pacing the kitchen, ripping at her fingernails, the phone pinched under her chin. In moments of crisis, she has always managed to lose herself in a cyclone of panic. Never keeps her head. He sighs, too loudly, sending a rush of wind into the phone. Jeanne falls silent.

Damn, he thinks. Christ. Now I've done it.

"Well, I'm *sorry*, Jack. I shouldn't have called you so late. I'm sorry. Never mind. Get back to what you were doing. Never mind me. We can talk in the morning."

"We'll find him, Jeannie," he hears himself saying, cutting her short. "We'll find him. He's just gone off to sow some wild oats. He's just been feeling full of himself, these days." As he goes on, Jack finds that he wants to believe himself. "He just went off for a little tour of the neighborhood. That's all, Jeannie. That's all. I promise. We'll find him tomorrow."

When he walks into the shop in the morning Jeanne is there already, red-eyed and red-nosed, leaves clinging to her jeans where she's been down on her hands and knees, checking under the porch and in the old spring box. She takes a step towards him, as if she is going to fall into his arms, then hesitates, bites her lip, collapses in a chair, and covers her face with her hands, letting out a muffled sob that hits Jack like a hammer in the chest.

They drive around all day doing twenty-five, Jeanne hanging half out the window, calling and whistling. "*Tiiiii-ny!*" It's a warm day, more September than December, and clouds of hatched gnats hover in the road.

Jeanne calls herself hoarse. Every so often Jack finds himself watching her heavy backside waggle as she strains out the window, then looks back quickly at the road, disturbed by it, vowing not to look again. At four o'clock they decide it's time to quit, without having found hair or hide of Tiny. Jeanne is crumpled against the door of the car as if she doesn't have the strength or the will to hold herself up. Jack feels utterly powerless.

When he drops her off back at the house, he grabs her hand before she gets out of the car and meets her eye. "You gonna be all right tonight?"

She bites her lip and nods.

"You call me if you need anything. You just pick up the phone and call. I'll put the phone right by the bed. All right?" He watches her go in and waits until she's closed the door behind her before he puts the car in gear.

Jack stops at the end of the drive, pops a pill, and eats a granola bar from the glove box. He is cramped up, exhausted, the small of his back aching and his glucose levels all out of whack. He feels hollow, nearly desolate. It can't just be the damn dog, he thinks, driving home. It's something else, something bigger.

They'd driven down roads they hadn't been on in years—past the old empty high school and the field where the drive-in used to be, now grown over with highbush honeysuckle and littered with junk cars, a few speakers still hanging off their posts like rotted teeth. It looked like a war field. Finished.

He stops and buys a pack of cigarettes—to hell with it, he

thinks, something else is going to quit long before my lungs do—aching for just some small physical pleasure to get him through the night. Before he leaves the gas station, though, feeling guilty, he shakes out three, leaving the rest of the pack on top of the trash can. Just as well, he thinks. Make some lucky sucker's day.

There is a place in Highland City that every generation thinks it is the first to discover. A gladelike swimming hole in the creek, set in a deep bowl of the hills. It's easy enough to get to from the road that you can bring in coolers and lawn chairs and cases of beer, but secluded enough that you can do anything you want out there and nobody's going to bother you. When Jack and Jeanne were kids everyone called it Valhalla, and spent their summer nights down there, when there wasn't something playing at the drive-in. I wonder what the kids call it now, Jack thinks, pulling into the rutted clearing off the side of the road. Probably nothing. These kids today have everything fed to them. No imagination.

Back in high school, Jeanne was always the first one in the water. Last one out, too. She was fearless then, even of the cottonmouths that scared everybody else off. She would stand in the creek, waist deep, splashing the water with her fingertips. "Jack! Jack!" she'd shout. "Get in here. Get your ass down here!"

He'd sit up on the bank with a beer and look at his friends. "Already got him on a chain," they would snicker to one another, and Jack would do his best to laugh along with them, crack another beer, and roll his eyes. He never went in, in order to prove something. Stupid reason not to go in, he thinks now. Should have.

He parks and pushes the seat all the way back, lights a cigarette. He closes his eyes and lets the smoke filter into his nostrils along with Jeanne's familiar smell, which lingers after their day in the car together. He tries to imagine that she is still sitting next to him, eighteen and in a wet bikini, smoking a cigarette and playing with the radio. In those days there was always something good on the radio.

After a while, feeling stiff and caged-in, Jack heaves himself out of the car and makes his way slowly into the trees, leaning hard on his cane. He starts down the hill, drawn by the smell of the leaves and the warm air that the woods still hold, and suddenly he can see the creek. It startles him—he remembers it being much deeper in the woods. He makes his way down to it and sits with difficulty on an old stump to light his second cigarette. The banks of the creek are worn smooth from years of bare feet, littered with beer cans and busted sneakers, fast food bags and old condoms. Jack shakes his head sadly. On a beech tree on the opposite bank, someone has spray-painted FUCK GOD.

He lets a drag linger in his lungs, feeling it creep in and fill all the corners. We had some days, he thinks. We did have some days. Back when we thought it was all ours for the taking. Back before everything got ruined. And it all got ruined at once. Funny how it happened that way. Just woke up one morning and there was no going back and fixing anything.

A pair of crows take off from a tree near him, the branch shaking. There's a feeling at the back of Jack's neck like someone is behind him. He turns around twice, scanning the purple-lit trees. Something pops in his shoulder the second time, a painful little explosion of nerves.

Ghosts, he thinks, rubbing his neck. Ha. What ghosts would bother to haunt these woods? Our teenage selves. The long hunters. Not angry ghosts or vengeful. No, just . . . disappointed.

He shifts his weight and looks around for a grave. They're all over these woods. His father taught him how to spot them: the depression in the ground that would be roughly the dimensions of a coffin, where the soil had settled over the years. "Always watch out for them," his father told him—walking across them disrespected the dead.

The long hunters buried each other in hollowed-out tree trunks, no time to build a proper coffin, no women to linger and weep over a grave. Scores of them must have died in these woods. A dangerous place, back then. But give me that over a hospital room any day, Jack thinks. Go with some dignity. And then, to be laid to rest the way so many creatures go: curled up in a log somewhere, tail over nose, and by spring they've crumbled into the log, and the log, in a few years, is crumbled into the soil. It makes him feel cheated and lonesome, looking up into the leaves, the bare crowns lit with the last of the sun. There's not a single tree left out here that would be big enough to hold him.

Take better care of yourself, the doctor told him, and there's no reason why you shouldn't live another thirty years. What the hell for? was Jack's first reaction. What's left? No grandbabies, no wife, no money to travel, and why did folks even bother to travel nowadays, when every place was just the same as the next?

Jeanne had wanted a baby. But those years, their chances, had disappeared in his drinking. He has only begun to regret this recently. I'm it, he thinks. The last of the Wells line. My work is all I'll leave the world. But some of the early work has already gone, popped at the seams, mice long since eaten the glue and made nests out of the stuffing. How long will the rest of it last? Longer. But not forever. For a while his mounts will hang in living rooms and hunting cabins and fathers will tell their sons, *That's a Jack Wells mount; he was the best, you know,* but after a generation or so no one will remember his name. And a few more decades down the road, he thinks, at the rate we're screwing it all up, what will it even matter? The water poisoned, the air ruined, too many damn people and more every day—what is it that we all want to hang around for, anyway?

Even the long hunters, Jack thinks, even they weren't smart enough. It only took a generation or two for them to foul it all up. The buffalo went first, then the birds. The fish, the deer, suddenly you couldn't just reach out and find dinner anymore. But what did it stop them? They just cut down the trees, built their frame houses, planted gardens and orchards, bought a few head of cattle. Went back up to Kentucky, came back with their children and wives.

The sun disappears. It gets cold. Jack shivers and suddenly wants to be home. He looks at the hill with great apprehension and lights his last cigarette, hands shaking, wondering if his brain will be able to send the proper messages to his muscles to get him back up. Hell. So what if I die out here? So I die out here. He tosses his butt into the creek and watches it float away, the water rippling over the smooth stones of the creek bed, resigning himself to the thought.

But who is he kidding? He wouldn't die out here. Instead he would spend a cold, painful, sleepless night huddled up under his jacket on the knobby roots and stones, and in the morning he'd have to piss on a rock, hobble up to the car, drive to the shop, take a dozen aspirin, and explain himself to Jeanne, who'd have been up all night calling, worried sick.

Jeanne.

I'm going. Just as soon as I catch my breath.

A car pulls in up at the clearing. The slam of doors. A radio. Kids. One of the voices breaks out from the crowd and carries down to the creek, a high manic laugh. *Ronnie.* Now I'm really going to have to explain myself, Jack thinks, but realizes it's possible that in the dark they did not see his car parked on the other side of the clearing. Maybe he can get up to it without them seeing him—if he skirts them and comes up on the other side. "Little punks," he says, heaves himself off the stump, and starts up the hill.

But his body doesn't want to cooperate. His muscles bicker and then wail and scream. His good knee seizes up. Every few steps he leans on his cane and tries to reason with his thighs. A low branch slices across his forehead, stinging his eyes.

"All right now, Jack," he tells himself, angry, gasping for breath. "This isn't Everest, you know."

After what seems like hours he gets far enough up the hill that he can see the clearing, the light of a fire they've built. Six or seven figures huddled in a ring around it. He sees Ronnie, then Tanya. She's sitting off to the side, her hands pulled up into her sleeves, drinking a can of beer. The beer makes her look young, just a little girl. The group seems to be discussing something. As he gets closer, there's a shift. They fall silent, slowly put down their beers.

"Shhh," he hears someone say.

"Did you hear that?"

"Listen. It's coming up from the creek."

Tanya stands up. Jack's heart swells a little, watching her up there, trying to see into the dark. Her face, lit by the fire, is filled with anticipation. Lips parted, her eyes dark in her pale face. Just pure and young and like anything might happen. She tucks her hair behind her ear and cocks her head.

Kids, Jack thinks again, fondly now. Suddenly he wants to speak to them, if they would only listen: I wish it was all going to turn out the way you think it will. I really do.

He looks down at the ground, then back up at them, wiping his eyes. You want a scare? He lets a branch snap under his good foot. That one's for you, Tanya. A gift. He sees her raise her hand, tentatively, as if to steady something. She puts her finger to her lips.

Jack smiles.

"It's . . . right . . . over . . . there," someone hisses. Ronnie stands up, poised, ready to run.

Jack gives the leaves a little rustle with his cane, forgetting the pain, starting to enjoy himself. And that's for you, Ronnie, you little S.O.B.

"That's it," Ronnie says. "I'm getting my gun." He turns and jogs towards the truck.

Jack feels a chill of fear. All right, all right! No guns, Ronnie, no guns—Jack takes a lurching step forward, about to shout, *Don't shoot*! But then he freezes. He holds his breath. Jack hears it—whatever it is—good Lord, he hears it, too.

Sweethearts of the Rodeo

Lately I've been thinking about that summer. We barely ever got off those ponies' backs. We painted war paint across their foreheads and pinned wild turkey feathers in our hair, whooped and raced across the back field, hanging on their necks. Some days they were a pair of bucking broncos, or unicorns, or circus horses, or burros on a narrow mountain pass. Other days they were regal as the ladies' horses, and we were two queens, veiled sultanas crossing the Sahara under a burning sky. We were the kidnapped maidens or the masked heroes. We braided flowers in their matted tails, dandelions and oxeye daisies that got lost in the snarls, wilted, and turned brown. We tore across the back field, our heels dug into their sides. We pulled them up short and did somersaults off their backs. We did handstands in the saddle. We turned on a dime. We jumped the triple oxer, the coop, the wall, the ditch. We were fearless. It was the summer we smoked our first cigarettes, the summer you broke your arm. It was the last summer, the last one before boys.

Our mothers drop us off every morning at seven. We grab two pitchforks and fly through our chores. For four dollars an hour we shovel loads of manure and wet shavings out of the stalls, scrub the water buckets, and fill the hayracks, the hay sticking to our wet T-shirts, falling into our shoes, our pockets, our hair. We race to see who can finish first. When we are thirsty, we run to the hose and drink. Late in the morning Curt comes out to the barn and leans against the massive sliding door. He wears sandals and baggy shorts, and under his thick, dark eyelashes, his eyes are rimmed with red. He tells us what other jobs there are to be done, that we must pick stones out of the riding ring, or refill the water troughs in the pasture with the long, heavy hose. We whine and stamp our feet. He is the caretaker, after all, and supposed to do these things himself.

We were just about to go riding, we say.

Girls, he says, winking. *Come on now.*

He looks over his shoulder and whistles for his dog. You stick your tongue out at his back. Some mornings he stays in his little house and doesn't come out until much later, when the ladies' expensive cars start pulling in the long driveway. They get out and lean against their shiny hoods, smoking cigarettes and talking to Curt in low voices. Sometimes only

one or two of them show up, and other times they all come at
once, a half-dozen of them with identical beige breeches and
high boots that we dream of at night. They never once get
a streak of manure across their foreheads or a water bucket
sloshed across their shirts. We turn down the volume of the
paint-splattered barn radio to hear what they're saying, but
we can't make it out. In the afternoon we eat the sandwiches
our mothers packed for us and throw our apple cores over
the fence to the ponies. They chew carefully and sigh in the
hot midday sun. Their eyes close and they let their pink-and-
gray mottled penises dangle. We go to them with soapy water
and a sponge in a bucket and clean the built-up crust from
their sheaths, reaching our arms far up inside. The ladies see
us doing this and pay us five dollars to do their geldings, then
stand by and watch us, wrinkling their perfect noses.

The ladies' horses all have brass name plates on their stall
doors, etched in fancy script, with the names of their sires
and dams in parentheses underneath. They are called Cu-
rator, Excelsior, Hadrian. The ponies' names change daily,
depending on the game. The ponies don't even have stalls.
They live out in the field where they eat all day under a cloud
of flies. Nobody remembers who they belong to. For the sum-
mer, they are ours. They are round and close to the ground,
wheezy and spoiled with bad habits. One is brown and dulled
by dust. The other is a pinto, bay with white splashes, white
on half his face, one eye blue, the other eye brown. The blue
eye is blind. We sneak up on this side when we go out to
the pasture to catch them, a green halter hidden behind your

back, a red one behind mine. The ponies let us get just close enough, then toss their heads and trot away. Peppermints and buckets of grain don't fool them. After a while, we learn to leave their halters on.

The grass in the pasture is knee-high, full of ticks and chiggers, mouse tunnels, quicksilver snakes that scare the ladies' horses into a frenzy. But not the ponies. They are un-spookable. Bombproof. When we cinch up their girths they twist their necks to bite our arms. They leave bruises like sunset-colored moons. As the summer gets hotter, we stop bothering with saddles altogether. We clip two lead lines to their halters, grab a hank of mane, and vault on.

We trot through the field and down the hill to the pine woods. We scramble up steep ridges. The ponies are barn sour, much faster coming home than going. We get as far away as we can and then give them their heads to race home through the woods, spruce limbs and vines whipping our faces. We know we are close when we can smell the manure pile. When we come up the hill it is looming like a dark mountain beside the barn. You make a telescope with your thumb and forefinger. Your fingernails are black to the quick. *Land ho!* you say. Crows land on the peak of the pile and send avalanches of dirty shavings down its sides. The ladies' little dogs jump out of the open windows of their cars and come running to us, tags jingling.

The ladies hardly ever ride. All day their horses stand out in the sun, their muscles like silk-covered stone. Some-times they bring them in to the barn and tie them up in the crossties, then wander into Curt's house and don't come out again. The horses wait patiently for an hour or so and then begin to paw and weave their heads. They can't reach the flies settling on their withers, the itches on their faces they want to rub against their front legs. They dance and swivel in the aisle, and still the ladies won't come out. Finally we unhook them from the ties and turn them back out in the pasture, where they spin and kick out a leg before galloping back to the herd. When the ladies come out of the little house, late in the afternoon, they squint in the light like they are coming out of a cave and don't ever seem to notice that their horses are not where they left them.

We do everything we can think of to torture Curt. Before he goes out to work on the electric fence, he switches off the fuse in the big breaker box in the barn. We sneak around and flip it back on, then hide and wait to hear his curses when he touches the wire. You slap me five. He comes back into the barn and flicks a lunge whip at us, and we giggle and jump. When he turns away we whisper, *I hate him.* With pitchforks we fling hard turds of manure in his direction, and he hooks his big arms around our waists and dumps us headfirst into the sawdust pile. We squeal and throw handfuls at him when he walks away. Oh, how we hate him! We pretend we've forgotten his name.

In the afternoon we ride our ponies close to the little house to spy on him. Their hooves make marks in the lawn like fingerprints in fresh bread. We ride as close as we dare and see things we don't see in our parents' houses: dirty laundry heaped in the hall, a cluster of dark bottles on top of the refrigerator, ashtrays and half-filled glasses crowding the kitchen table, which is just a piece of plywood on two sawhorses. Your pony eats roses from the bushes under the windows. He wears a halo of mosquitoes. From the bedroom we hear voices, Curt's and a lady's, but it is the only room in which the blinds have been pulled. We try to peer through the cracks, but the ponies yank at their bits and dance in the rosebushes, and we don't really want to see, anyway. *Come on,* you say, and we head out to the back field to play circus acrobats, cops and robbers, cowboys and Indians, whatever mood happens to strike us this day.

The ponies bear witness to dozens of pacts and promises. We make them in the grave light of late day, with every intention of keeping them. We cross our hearts and hope to die on the subjects of horses, husbands, and each other. We dare each other to do near-impossible things. You dare me to jump from the top of the manure pile, and I do, and land on my feet, with manure in my shoes. I double-dare you to take the brown pony over the triple oxer, which is higher than his ears. You ride hell-bent for it but the pony stops dead, throwing you over his head, and you sail through the air and land in the rails, laughing. We are covered in scrapes and bruises, splinters buried so deep in our palms that we don't know they are there. Our bodies forgive us our risks, and the ponies do, too. We have perfected the art of falling.

.   .   .

We know every corner of the barn, every loose board, every shadow, every knot in the wood. It is old and full of holes, home to many things: bats and lizards and voles, spiders that hang cobwebs in the corners like hammocks, house sparrows that build nests in the drainpipes with beakfuls of hay until one day a dead pink baby bird drops to the feet of one of the ladies, who screams and clutches her hair. You scoop it up and toss it on the manure pile, and Curt comes out with the long ladder and pours boiling water down the pipe, and that is the end of the sparrows. Curt laughs at the lady, and rolls his eyes behind her back, and winks at us. We wink back. There is a fly strip in the corner that quivers with dying flies. When it is black with bodies and bits of wing, it is our job to replace it, and we hold our breath when we take it down, praying it won't catch in our hair. And then there are the rats, so many rats that we rip from glue boards and smash with shovels, or pull from snap traps and fling into the woods, or find floating in water troughs where they've dragged themselves, bellies distended with poison and dying of thirst.

In the basement is the workbench where Curt never works; above it, rusty nails sit in a line of baby food jars with lids screwed into a low beam. The manure spreader is parked down there in the dark, like a massive shamed beast. When we open the trap door in the floor above to dump loads from our wheelbarrows, a rectangle of light illuminates the mound of dirty shavings and manure, and we see mice scurry over it like currents of electricity. The ladies never go down to the basement. It is there that we sometimes sit to discuss them, comparing their hair, their mouths, the size of their breasts. *Did you see that one throw up behind the barn Friday afternoon? Did you see this one's diamond ring? Did you see that one slip those pills into Curt's shirt pocket, smiling at him? What were they?*

We hear them call their husbands' offices on the barn telephone and say they are calling from home. We watch two or three go into the little house together, shutting the door behind them. We see Curt stagger from the house and fall over in the yard and stay where he falls, very still, until one of the ladies comes out and helps him up, laughing, and takes him back inside. The ladies hang around when the farrier comes, a friend of Curt's with blond hair and a cowboy hat, watching as he beats a shoe to the shape of a hoof with his hammer. He swears as he works and we stand in the shadows by the grain room and listen carefully, cataloguing every new word. When he leaves, one or two ladies ride off with him in his truck and return an hour or so later and go back to what they had been doing, as if they had never left. They lock themselves in the tack room and fill it with strange-smelling smoke. When we sit in the hayloft we hear their voices below us, high and excited, like small children. The ladies wear lipstick in the morning that is gone by the afternoon. They wear their sunglasses on cloudy days. Some mornings we see that the oil drum we use for empty grain bags is filled to the top with beer bottles. We watch them, and the rules that have been strung in our heads like thick cables fray and unravel in a dazzling arc of sparks. Then we climb on the ponies' backs and ride away down the hill.

One afternoon Curt gives us each a cigarette, and laughs as we try to inhale. *Look, girls!* he says, striking a match on the sole of his boot and lighting his own. *Like this.* We watch his face as he takes a drag, his jaw shadowed with a three-day beard. Later we steal two more from his pack and ride into the woods to practice, watching each other and saying, *No, like this! Like this!* We put Epsom salts in Curt's coffee and lock the tack room door from the inside. We steal his baseball cap and manage to get it hooked on the weathervane. *Ha!* we say, and spit on the ground. *Take that!* He throws one of his flip-flops at us. He drags us shrieking to the courtyard and sprays us with the hose. He tells us we stink. We tell him we don't care.

There is one horse worth more money than the rest put together—it was brought over on a plane, all the way from England. One day we are sitting up in the hayloft, sucking through a bag of peppermints and discussing all the horses we will own someday when we hear an animal's scream from below. The horse, left tied and standing in the aisle, has spooked and broken its halter, gashed its head open on a beam. Blood drips off its eyelashes to a pool by its hooves and it sways like a suspension bridge. We grab saddle pads from the tack room, the ladies' expensive fleece ones, and press them to the wound. They grow hot and heavy with blood.

It runs down our arms, into our hair. The horse shakes its head, gnashes its teeth at us. We look over at the little house, all the blinds drawn tight. Who will knock on the door? Who will go? We flip a coin. I don't remember if you won or lost, but you are the one who cuts through the flower bed, who stands on the step and knocks and knocks, and after a long time Curt comes out in jeans and bare feet, no shirt. I hide in the bushes and watch. *What?* he says, frowning. You point at his crotch and say, *XYZ!* Without looking down he zips his fly in one motion, like flipping on a light switch. And then in the shadow of the doorway is the lady who the horse belongs to, scowling, her blond hair undone, looking at you like she is having a hard time understanding why you are covered in blood. After the vet comes and stitches up the wound she looks at us suspiciously and whispers to Curt. Later, he makes sure she is within earshot before scolding us. When the vet has left and they have gone back into the house, we knock down a paper wasps' nest and toss it through the back window of her car.

There is a pond in the back pasture where the horses go to drink, half hidden by willows and giant honeysuckle bushes that shade it from the noonday sun. On the hottest days we swim the ponies out to the middle, and when their hooves leave the silty bottom, it feels like we are flying. The water is brown and rafts of manure float past us as we swim, but we don't care. We pretend the ponies are Pegasus. And as they swim, we grow quiet thinking about the same thing. We think about Curt—his arms, the curve of his hat brim, the way he smells when he gets off the tractor in the afternoon. You trail your hand in the water and say, *What are you thinking about?* And I say, *Nothing.* When we come out of the water the insides of our thighs are streaked with wet horsehair, as if we are turning into centaurs or wild beasts. The ponies shake themselves violently and we jump off as they drop to their knees to roll in the dust. Other days it is too hot to even swim, to move at all. We lie on the ponies' necks as they graze in the pasture, our arms hanging straight down. The heat drapes across our shoulders and thighs. School is as incomprehensible as snow.

Rodeo is our favorite game, because it is the fastest and most reckless, involving many feats of speed and bravery, quick turns, trick riding. One day late in July, out in the back field, we decide to elect a rodeo clown and a rodeo queen. The ponies stamp out their impatience while we argue over who will be what. Finally the games begin. There is barrel racing and bucking broncos and the rodeo parade. We discover that we can make the ponies rear on command by pushing them forward with our heels while we hold the reins in tight. *Yee haw!* we say, throwing one arm up in the air. The ponies chew the bit nervously as we do it over and over again. We must lean far forward on their necks, or we will slip off. Then the pinto pony goes up and you start to lose your balance. I am doubled over laughing until I see you grope for the reins as the pony goes high, and you grab them with too much effort, and yank

his head back too far. He hangs suspended for a moment be-
fore falling backward like a tree on his spine. You disappear
as he rolls to his side, and reappear when he scrambles to
his feet, the reins dangling from the bit. I jump off my pony
and run to you. Your arm, from the looks of it, is broken.
Oh shit, I say. You squint up at me through a veil of blood.
Doesn't hurt.

Curt was the one who rescued you. He drove his pickup
through the tall grass of the back pasture, lifted you onto
the bench seat, made you a pillow with his shirt. And when
he couldn't get ahold of your parents, he was the one who
drove you to the emergency room. I rode in the truck bed,
and watched through the window as you stretched your
legs across his lap, your bare feet on his thighs. I could
see his arms, your face, his tanned hand as he brushed
the hair, or maybe tears, from your eyes. I sat across from
him at the hospital, waiting while they stitched the gash
on your forehead and put your left arm in a cast, and I
came in with him to check on you. I hung back in the cor-
ner when he leaned over the table, and I heard you whisper
to him in a high, helpless voice. I watched your hand grope
out from under the blanket, reaching towards his. And I
saw him hold it. He held it with both hands. Of course I
was jealous, and still am. You must still have that scar to
remind you of that summer. I have nothing I can point to,
nothing I can touch.

It was early in August when the brown pony died. It happened overnight, and no one knew how: whether he colicked and twisted his gut, or had a heart attack, or caught a hind foot in his halter while tending an itch and broke his own neck. When we found the body, we didn't cry. I remember that we weren't even very sad. We went to find Curt, who lit a cigarette and told us not to tell the ladies. Then we went back and looked at the pony's still body, his velvety muzzle, his open eye, his lips pulled back from his big domino teeth. We touched his side, already cold. Later we rode the pinto pony double out to the pond, your arms around my waist, your cast knocking against my hipbone. Behind us the tractor coughed as Curt pulled the pony's body to the manure pile with heavy chains. We slipped off the pinto, letting him wander away, and sprawled out in the grass. You scratched inside your cast with a stick. Grasshoppers sprang around us. We lay there all afternoon and into the evening, your head on my stomach, our fingers in the clover, trying to think up games we could play with only one pony.

Weeks later we were alone in the barn. We were sweeping the long center aisle, pressing push brooms towards one another from opposite ends, the radio flickering on and off, like it always did. When it faded out completely, we heard the squabbling of dogs out back. We dropped our brooms and ran to see what they'd got. Through a cloud of dust in the paddock we could make out Curt's dog, his butt to us, bracing himself with his tail in the air and growling at one of the ladies' fierce little dogs, who was shaking his head violently, his eyes squeezed shut. Between them, they had the brown pony's head. It took awhile to recognize it. It was mostly bone, yellow teeth and gaping eye sockets, except for a few bits of brown hair that hung on the forehead, some cheek muscle and stringy tendon clinging to the left side. And then we saw the little scrap of green against the white: the pony still had his halter on. This was what the dogs had got their teeth around. Curt had never bothered to take it off. With a final shake of his jaws, the little dog managed to snatch the pony's head away, and he dragged it around the corner of the barn, Curt's dog bounding after.

We stood in the slanting September light and watched this. We listened to the dogs' whines and rumblings, the scrape of the skull against the ground. Then we picked up our brooms, and when we were done sweeping we went and got the pinto pony and rode double down the hill and didn't think much about it again. Death was familiar that summer. It was in the road, in the woods, in the holes of the foundation of the barn; it was the raccoon rotting in the ditch, and the crows that settled there to pick at it until they, too, were flattened by cars, and their bodies swelled and stank in the heat; it was the half-decayed doe we found in the woods with maggots stitching in and out of its flesh, the stillborn foal wrapped in a rotting amniotic sac in the pasture where the vultures perched. We caught a whiff of it, sniffed it out, didn't flinch, touched it with our bare hands, ate lunch immediately afterwards. We weren't frightened of death.

And a few summers later, spinning out of control on a loose

gravel road in a car full of boys and beer, we weren't scared of it then, either, and we laughed and said to the boy at the wheel, *Do it again*. We only learned to fear it later, much later, when we realized it knew our names and, worse, the name of everyone we loved. At the height of the summer, in the very dog days, I would have said that we loved the ponies, but I realize now we never did. They were only everything we asked them to be, and that summer, that was enough. I don't know. Lately I've been thinking someone should write an elegy for those ponies. But not me.

The Still Point

In Thunderbird, Illinois, I get to thinking the world is going to end. During the day it's cotton candy and caramel apples, the Howler and the Zipper, the looping soundtrack of the carousel. But at night, when I'm stretched out in the back of the truck on the outskirts of Camper City, trying to sleep in the bowl of quiet left by five hundred people gone home sunburned and broke to their beds, the feeling sneaks in and sits down square on my chest: these are the last days. It's all going to break up. It's as if I'm eavesdropping on the secret that history has been whispering to itself all along: the punch line, the trick ending, the big joke. I curl up alongside the wheel well, wondering why I'm the only one who hears it. But morning always comes, daylight burning through the windows, the truck hot as a greenhouse, and I slide out barefoot onto the grass for another slow drag around the sun.

Across the aisle, Dub leans out the door of his camper, shading his eyes and squinting in my direction. "Hurry it up, man, hurry your ass up," he shouts. "They're calling for rain today."

He steps out of his camper as if he's lowering himself into a pool, gripping the doorframe and easing himself down on one leg, then the other. It takes a while for him to wade his way over. I pull off my T-shirt and crack my neck. The morning is hot and damp as the inside of a dog's mouth. All around us, Camper City wakes up slow. Generators hum, people light their first smokes of the day, piss out the door. The Haunted House woman puts on the radio and steps out to do her exercises under the awning of her RV, bouncing in a tank top, touching her toes. Everyone struggles to maintain something of a routine. Me, every morning, I remind myself where we are. Now: Illinois. I say it out loud, to make it official.

By the time Dub makes it over he's sweating and puffing, his mouth a deflated O. He presses a hand to my back window to steady himself. "Get a move on," he wheezes. "We'll get an early crowd. Rain in the afternoon. They're all at home right now, glued to the Weather Channel, changing their plans. I guarantee."

Dub is always guaranteeing the unguaranteeable: the weather, the whims of people, the quality of questionably constructed merchandise. A born hustler. Me, I couldn't sell a drowning man a life jacket. We could get no business at all, for what I care. I'd just as soon sit at my table and watch the crows tear around above me, wondering what the hell set down in the center of their field. But still, I'm pulling on a shirt, lacing up my boots. Illinois. Really it's just another sky, another field, another morning, another sea of faces to come, blank-eyed, slack-jawed, hands on wallets, not as much to see the spectacle as to take something away from it to put up on the shelf.

"Coffee?" Dub jerks his thumb back at the camper, jowls swaying. I nod and slam the tailgate shut. Five months, four thousand miles, Dub's coffee has been slowly hollowing out my gut. He is a friend, or at least constant as one.

"Christ, it better hold," he shouts on his way back to the camper, shaking his finger at the sky. "I sure as hell can't afford a slow day."

Twenty minutes later, the coffee cranking through me, I head up to the port-a-johns on the midway. Up here, things are slow to creak into gear: the carnies fold tarps, run patchy safety checks on rides, shout to one another in English, Spanish, Portuguese. Sodas are plunged into ice at the concessions stands, hot dogs are eaten for breakfast, no buns. The old man in the cotton candy stand wearily starts his centrifuge spinning and shakes his cartons of pink sugar. Ed the Giant Steer, led out of his tent so that it can be flea-bombed for the second time in two weeks, sways on his stilt legs and groans, yanking his lead in his handler's palms, diving for the grass. A heavy roll of ADMIT ONE tickets is dropped in the dust and rolls to a stop at my feet. No one looks up when I pass. I might as well be just another faceless customer, passing through. The outfit is watertight. Us hucksters, relegated to the side strips, we're nothing but gulls following a fishing boat, swooping in to snatch the leavings.

Most of the vendors down on the back side are already at their booths, counting out money, listening to radios. Yawning, sleep still burning off, looking only half-ready for the droves. I nod to the few I know: Indian Jim, who sells five-dollar sunglasses and isn't Indian in the least, Danny, the kid, sizzling on pills even at this hour, with his dream catchers and blown-glass beads on cords. They nod back, eyes hard.

I stop at the wing stand to say hello to Kathy. She leans out on the counter with her hands clasped in front of her and smiles big and blank, like she's waiting to take my order.

"Cole, baby," she says.

"Good goddamn morning," I say.

Kathy's hair, as always, is done in two braids, a hairstyle she must have outgrown forty years ago. No makeup yet, which makes a big difference. She's wearing a low-necked T-shirt covered with sequins that catch the light and send it sparking all over the place. I can see the tops of her breasts, brown and cooked-looking. Whenever I see them in the light of day, I can't imagine how I ever find comfort there.

"Think the weather will hold?" she says. Her bracelets jangle as she waves towards the sky. I squint up at the clouds, making out like I'm studying something she can't see.

"Yes," I say. "Guaranteed."

She laughs, too loud. "You getting into anything tonight?" Next to the deep fryer, turkey drumsticks and wings are lined up, ruddy and stoic-looking, as if they're steeling themselves for the hot oil. Dinosaur Wings, they call them. There's a pterodactyl on the sign in the window: BOB AND KATHLEEN DENNIS. PROUDLY SERVING YOU.

"What's today?" I say, though we both know it makes no difference. Every day is the same. Every night, the same clamor to erase it.

She thinks for a minute, her lips moving, counting back. "Saturday," she finally says, flipping a braid over her shoulder, triumphant.

"One more day. Tomorrow we go."

"Where?" she says with a sigh. "I don't ask anymore."

"West. Over the river." For weeks I've been looking forward to it, crossing the Mississippi, thinking things will be different on the other side. But as soon as I say it, all my anticipation fades, the way a trout loses color when it is yanked out of the water.

"Come by the bus this afternoon and see me," she says and winks, then swipes at the counter with a rag and turns to the crackling fryer. "Bob takes over at four."

When I get down to my table, Dub's already in his tent across the way, refolding and restacking T-shirts. The tent is packed with them, most XL or larger, stiff with silk-screened designs: women in Confederate flag thongs leaning across the hoods of Ford and Chevy trucks, bloody-fanged pit bulls in studded collars, Uncle Sam with his middle finger extended above an American flag and the message THESE COLORS DON'T RUN. A 'Nam buddy left him a warehouse full in his will. Dub's been on the road two years now, says he'll quit when he sells them all. But I don't know. There's a point of no return, I'm beginning to think, and Dub may have passed it several thousand miles back.

I've been traveling since spring. Already the highway has become the one true thing, towns only stopovers, names on signs. Certain smells, clouds, movements of trees will once in a while feel exactly like home. Shadows will fall on the road in such a familiar way that I get disoriented and think I'm back in Virginia, headed down to the farm, where everything is still as it once was, and a certain sort of peace will come over me. Then the light shifts and it all shatters.

I pull out my boxes, roll up my tarp, and set up my table: blue glass medicine jars, tin toys, old coins, moldy magazines and tools. Wherever I go, I'm always knocking on farmhouse doors, offering to clean out old couples' sheds and barns. All I need is some bleach and a wire brush, and people will pay fifty bucks for an old milk pail, a Red Flyer with a broken axle. ANTIQUES, my sign says. Dub is always pointing it out to people, laughing. "Antiques? He sells junk. I sell trash." Business is generally slow. I'm lucky enough to get Dub's runoff, wives who wander over while their husbands are clawing through piles of T-shirts, debating if the woman astride the John Deere tractor is better in blonde or brunette.

I hear Dub shout my name and look up, annoyed. What now? "Looky here!" he's saying. He's standing in the door of his tent, waving me over. In his hand I see something hanging from a chain, glinting. When I get over there he holds it out against his palm for me to see: a girl's necklace, a tiny gold heart, nearly swallowed up in his beefy hand.

"Where'd you get it?" I say, suspicious.

He taps the side of his nose. "Found it on my way over here. Sniffed it out." His eyes are glassy from the heat, his forehead glistening. He's got half a pound of shrapnel in his left calf and thigh. Walking, standing, everything takes its toll. He pulls out a folding chair and sits down heavily, grunting. "Hell," he says, grinning like a dog. "I think it's worth something, too." He grabs my hand and pours the chain into it. "Go on, man. Take it. Sell it."

I look down at the little heart. Why not? Everything else on my table is borrowed, begged, stolen from the dead. When I go back and lay it down among the old campaign buttons and souvenir pen knives, it might as well be a relic of someone long gone from this world.

Six months ago, my twin brother Clay's comic books were the first things I sold. Our house and pastures went to a development company after two days on the market, every penny paying for my mother's new apartment in the center with round-the-clock care. Her mind, by then, was as twisted and looped as a tattered curtain in a dark window. It was up to me to clear out the house. Clay's room, fifteen years after his death, was exactly as he'd left it, untouched for nearly as many years as he'd been alive. Opening his door stirred up the dust that had settled in his absence, made it gleaming, glaring, new again. It was another day before I could bring myself to go in, and even then, I moved around like a trespasser, as if any minute he might appear in the doorway. I found the comic books boxed up carefully, chronologically, under his bed. A brittle piece of notebook paper, left over from the days when we fought over everything, fluttered to the floor when I lay on my stomach to pull them out: *Hands off, Cole!* But that money kept me going for months, bought me the truck, got me miraculously, against all odds, out of Virginia—*Spider-Man, The Fantastic Four, Green Lantern, Atomic Man.*

The people come, as they always do. In spite of the heat, the humidity, the exhaust-colored sky, they come dropping coins and car keys, yanking kids along by the wrists, eating funnel cake with their eyes on the Ferris wheel, their dogs locked in hot cars. I sit behind the table and watch them, the same faces making the rounds, hell-bent like they're searching for something. It's always the same, everywhere. I watch boys and men clamor in Dub's tent, T-shirts in their fists, throwing their money at him. I hear the clang of the bell at the Test Your Strength booth, the shouts of the barkers, hollers from the rickety Tempest, screams from the Gravitron every time the floor drops. The bleeps and buzzes and techno bass beats of the games. Eyes pass over my table and move on, looking for something bright and new. A hot air balloon rises on the horizon, hovers red and stark against the steel-gray sky. People stop to point it out to one another, causing traffic jams on the paths. Something about it makes me uneasy. It looks like it has come to judge us.

No one has stopped at my table by the time the smells of lunch start to waft over: corn dogs, sausage and onions, Dinosaur Wings. At night, the smell is deep in Kathy's braids. Bob doesn't want her anymore, or at least that's what she told me. He spends hours in the wing stand after closing, trying to teach himself guitar. Kathy sits in the bus and waits for me. I come because there's nowhere else to go. She has an easy laugh, the optimism of youth. Bob's missing two fingers. He curses the stubs when he plays, the chords muted and muddy. The bus is parked so close behind the stand that sometimes, in bed with her, I can hear him. I pull the blanket over our heads and try not to listen. When I listen, I start to sink through the dark depths towards the pointlessness of it all. Why does he bother? At his age, what's the use?

Last night, I left the bus late and ended up at the grandstand, where most of the crowd had gathered for a beauty pageant. It was part of some festival going on in conjunction with the fair: the Corn Festival, the Harvest Festival, the Illinois Pride Festival, I don't know what. The girls, in their elaborate dresses, all looked incredibly earnest and downright scared, as if this was the most important event of their lives. The winner cried as the judges crowned her, touching her frothy pink dress and piled-up hair. The sash they looped over her shoulders read MISS HOPEWELL COUNTY. She twisted it in her fingers as she stepped to the microphone to give a speech about her brother in the army. "We never know when the enemy might strike," she said, feedback crackling. "It could happen right here in Thunderbird. That's why I'd like to take a moment of silence for our boys over there. They remind us all to follow our dreams and never give up." The heads in the grandstand all nodded, and after a round of applause there was a minute or two of an almost sacred quiet. Out there on the edge of the crowd, I tried to direct my own silence towards the common cause, but all those grave unmoving faces only made me feel more invisible and alone.

Afterwards she posed for pictures, biting her lip between smiles. As she turned and waved to the crowd, she moved like so many country girls I know: trying to fold in on herself, trying to tuck away her broad muscular shoulders like wings. I thought about the girls Clay and I ran with in Virginia, girls who seemed to hold the answer to a question we hadn't yet learned to ask. Clay was the one they liked, though we were as near identical as two people could be. The only difference was that he had half an inch on me, a birthmark on his right shoulder, and a heart so big all the girls thought he was in love with them. He'd take them all out driving, that nightmare summer he was killed in the accident, the summer we turned sixteen. The age this girl must be, the age I last felt whole.

I saw her again, late, past midnight. The rides shut down, the games closing up, most people gone home, I walked out into the field, far out to where I could turn and see the midway lights from a distance. Already thinking about packing up the truck, slamming the tailgate shut on everything I own. At night I like to do this, imagine the field once we've left it: the deer coming out of the woods, noses working over crumpled napkins, the foxes creeping out onto the trampled paths, sawdust scattering in the wind. It's usually a comfort, knowing the field will recover without a trace of us, just days after we're gone. But there's a danger to picturing a place without you in it. After a while you can start to feel like nothing at all.

When I walked back up towards Camper City, I went past the grandstand again, empty now. By the bleachers, I happened to notice a teddy bear. It was bright orange, a prize off a game, glowing a little in the dirt. It reminded me of something, and I almost bent to pick it up, but then I heard them. A scuffling like animals, a hollow sound as she banged against the bleachers. When I peered into the darkness it took a few seconds to make sense of it. She had changed out of her pink dress and into a pair of jean shorts, which were down around her knees. But she was still wearing her sash, crooked now, flapping like she was unraveling. He was behind her, hands in her hair, yanking her head back a little with each thrust, his big white T-shirt billowing. I stood there and watched the whole thing, nothing but a pair of eyes. It was over fast. When he let go she didn't move, just stayed there hanging on the support strut of the bleachers, then slowly bent down and picked up the bear and tenderly brushed off the dirt.

I stepped into the shadow of a ticket booth as he turned and zipped his fly. I couldn't see his face, but I recognized the shirt immediately. It was one of Dub's—THE HUNTER'S NIGHT-MARE—a deer riding an ATV with a rifle strapped across its shoulders, a dead man in camo tied to the back.

Five months on the road and already I've seen too much. Too much to feel any shred of hope for the long-gone world. I feel the burden of it all clattering behind me, slowing me down, like cans tied on for a honeymoon. Sometimes I wonder why it hasn't all burned up or broken down already. Sometimes it makes me want to lie down right where I am and just let the grass grow over me.

The sky, by two, is yellow and angry. A wash of worried murmurs moves through the crowd. Mothers peer up at the bloated clouds, clutching raincoats, old men mutter and tell their wives they're ready to go home. Little kids run shrieking down the path, oblivious. I sell a chipped butter crock to a blue-haired, heavy-faced woman with white plastic shopping bags strung along her arms like buoys. "What'll you all do if it rains?" she asks, swinging her head towards the midway, bags rustling. She widens her eyes in concern, as if she can think of no more terrible a fate.

I look up, ready to be done with these people, put Thunderbird in the rearview as I tear off down the road. "Same thing as you," I say, snapping the money box closed. "Get wet."

It is only a legend, the Thunderbird. A myth the settlers stole from the Indians to scare little boys out of venturing too far from home. But they told the story enough times that they started to believe it themselves. Started whispering the terrible *what if*s, started to keep an eye on the sky. Always watching for the dark shape in the trees that might be waiting to swoop down and carry their children away. A hundred years ago, two traveling men pulled into town proclaiming they had captured the beast, that they had it alive and caged in a tent, to be viewed for two bits admission. When the crowd gathered, one of them went around collecting money, working the people up, describing the creature's great ferocity, the size and crushing strength of its talons and beak. And then just at the moment before the unveiling, the other one came running out from behind the tent, screaming, "It's escaped! Run for your lives!" And in the pandemonium that followed, they packed it all up quick and took off for the next town. Dub told me the story, doubled up with laughter. "You'd think that would have put an end to it," he said. But every year, even now, there are one or two more sightings. I can imagine it, looking out at the mute woods: how you might think you have glimpsed a wing or a passing shadow, the shuddering near-miss of catastrophe.

I know how they felt, those travelers: telling the same story town after town, the faces and the story must have eventually blurred, so they no longer knew what was hoax and what was truth.

I'm ready to take a break, clear my head, walk away for a while, when a group of teenagers comes careening down the path and slides to a stop in front of Dub's tent. Three boys in low-slung jeans jab a pink cloud of cotton candy in one another's faces, laughing and bumping into people. With them, in tight jeans and a tank top but still in her sash and crown, is Miss Hopewell County, giggling and slapping at their arms, trying to get in the middle of it all. She looks over and catches my eye, flashes a smile. I look down and grind my fist into my thigh. Sixty-six thousand miles an hour, the earth whips around the sun, while girls like this brush their hair, paint their nails, call their friends, believe that it all revolves around them. Suddenly she's in front of me, shimmering in the heat, still with that center-of-the-universe smile.

"Hey," she says.

"Hello," I say through my teeth. I can see the top of her bra as she leans over the table—lacy, white, expectant.

"Cool," she says, reaching to touch an old pillbox hat. Up close, her face has a blank innocence, like a field ready for the plow. She probably still thinks that one of those boys is going to sweep her off her feet, carry her away from here.

She gasps. "My necklace," she says, her hand flying to her throat. She looks up at me with big blinking eyes. "Where'd you find it?"

I look over her shoulder at the boys, who seem to have tired of their game, and are standing around like cows, gazing dumbly at the horizon. I wonder which one wrapped his fingers in her hair last night, leaned her up against the bleachers. Which one might do it tonight. A meanness takes hold of me.

"What are you talking about?" I say, still looking at the boys.

"That's my locket. I lost it last night. I've been looking for it all day." *All day.* She says it with a suffering sigh, as if a day was an interminable amount of time, as if we lived on a giant planet that turned infinitely slowly around the sun. Under my clothes, all the humidity of the air collects, heating up.

"What a coincidence," I say, "that I've got one just like it. I've had this one for months." My face burns. Sweat breaks. I squeeze my hands together behind my back, fighting the urge to pull off my shirt.

"But it's mine," she says, trying to laugh. I can see she has decided I must be teasing her. She's a little drunk, lining her words up carefully, like she's placing them on a tightrope. "Here," she says, reaching for it. "I can prove it." I find myself grabbing her hand and pushing it back from the table. Startled, she jerks it away.

"It's forty-five bucks," I say. Willing her, just willing her, to go away.

"But it's mine. If you look—"

"Forty. I can go as low as forty." I wipe sweat from my face with the back of my hand. I'm wet all over now, my clothes clinging to me, sweat running down my face. "Afraid I can't go any lower than that."

"It's mine," she says again, but quietly, dazed, with the voice of a little girl. Suddenly I can see her bedroom, in a brick ranch on the edge of her daddy's cornfield. Her mother closing the drapes and turning on the lamps every afternoon at five, though the sun is still throwing wild light across the corn. I feel a wave of sympathy. She must think it will never change.

She turns and looks back at the boys. "Who are you, anyway?" she says with her head turned, her voice filling with tears. But it's clear I've won. Without looking back, she goes over to the boys and disappears into the pack as they slouch up towards the midway.

The inside of my mouth, fingertips, toes, everything's buzzing, ringing, like I've just come crashing back down through the atmosphere. As soon as they're out of sight, I lay my hand flat over the necklace, close my fingers around it, and slip it in my back pocket.

On the drive in two days ago, I stopped at a historical marker, just to break up the numbness of the unbroken fields along the road. It was a plaque about the Hopewell people, who thousands of years ago lived on this land and built ceremonial earthworks, great burial mounds where they laid their dead to rest along with pottery, crude figurines, and stone tools. And there it was across the field, the mound, nothing spectacular about it at all. I got out of the truck and walked over, thinking it might be more impressive up close. There were daffodils growing along the sides of it, and a beer can had rolled down from the top. I picked it up and stood there and tried to feel some sense of the sacred, of the permanence. But I felt nothing, just the late blankness of an August afternoon, a plane droning overhead. Then, as I stood there flexing the can under my thumb, the loneliness of the ages suddenly grazed past—the shards of clay pots and bits of stone blades, the bottles and cans of countless teenage parties, the boxes of silverware and reading glasses and overcoats that I am always hauling out of other people's attics—all the things people leave behind, and how they really can tell us nothing, nothing about a life lived, nothing about an entire civilization that has disappeared from the face of the earth. I pictured some future race, trying to make sense of what will be left of us, all of our precious treasures sad and useless in the rubble and ruin. It flashed past with a ringing in my ears, left me staggering with irrelevance. Then I let the beer can fall and walked back to the truck, the miles ahead stretching out before me like a staircase that leads nowhere.

The rain starts at four. Slow, just a drizzle, and people duck under shelter to wait, not wanting to go home. After a while, they begin to venture back out, holding plastic bags over their heads. Umbrellas bloom in the pathways. The Mexicans come down from the midway and shake straw over the churned-up ground, kick at the power cords, giving each other dark, dubious looks. The Ferris wheel keeps turning in the grizzled air. Someone hits the jackpot up at B–52 Breakdown, the lights flash and the sirens wail, and everyone freezes for a minute, their faces full of alarm, as if the unthinkable has happened. They laugh nervously when they realize their mistake, take another bite of their hot dogs, keep making the rounds.

All afternoon I've been slipping my hand into my back pocket, pressing my thumb against the point of the necklace's heart. Just to feel the dull prick, just to be sure it is still there. I keep searching the revolving faces, hoping and dreading that she might streak by. Her tight jeans would be soaked now, her hair wet, the white satin sash flashing behind her. I wonder if she would stop again. I want her to stop again. I know exactly what I would say: *You don't want it.*

But after a while I start to get cold, my jeans heavy and wet, the rain feeling like it's seeping through me. I unfold the tarp over the table and go to Dub's to wait it out. It's crowded in the tent, warm with bodies. I drop into the folding chair in the corner and watch the people jostle one another, grabbing for shirts. I lift one off the pile closest to me. THE HUNTER'S NIGHTMARE. What the boy under the bleachers was wearing. My stomach clenches.

"Hey, Dub," I shout across the chaos. "Where'd you get that necklace?"

"What necklace?" he calls back, looking up from his cash register as he hands someone his change.

"Come on," I say, no patience for this.

He ignores me, stuffing half a dozen shirts in a bag. The deer on the shirt looks at me with a near-human face. It strikes me as the most indecent thing I've ever seen. I hold it halfway up. "How can you sell this garbage?" I say, loud, trying to turn some heads.

Dub, unfazed, looks over. "I don't have to," he shouts over the din. "It sells itself." Several customers' eyes widen when they see the shirt in my hand, and they elbow their way over to get a better look. I let it fall back down on the table and push my chair back. Dub comes over and grabs it. "Made in Malaysia, man. Only the finest." He throws it to a fat ten-year-old, whose face jiggles when he catches it. "Come on, Cole, where's your sense of humor?"

"I think I lost it somewhere back in Ohio," I say.

"Under the bleachers," he says. "But now I'm giving away all my secrets."

I hang around at my table another half hour, not know-ing what else to do. The rain keeps coming, falling in big, heavy drops, and it must be apparent to even the most op-timistic that it's not going to stop. A distant clap of thunder sounds. The crowd is steadily thinning, and finally I give up on it. I pack up my table, wrapping things haphazardly in newspapers and rags, throw all of it in my crates. I see Dub shoo a pack of boys out of his tent, and they pull up the hoods of their sweatshirts and head doggedly back up to the midway, determined, like soldiers. He stands at the door with his palm stretched out and makes a face at me that says he's quitting too. "I got a pocket full of dead presidents," he shouts. "I ain't complaining."

I shove my crates under the table and tie down the tarp. I'm ready for the warmth of Kathy's bus, the sterile, off-the-lot smell of it, the huge leather couch that slides out from the wall at the press of a button. As I head up the paths, I see that the only people left on them are teenagers. The only ones willing to get soaked to the bone for one last go on the Tempest or Zipper, now that there are no lines. They're still eating hot dogs and funnel cake off soggy paper plates. I reach into my pocket, touch the necklace, and wonder if she's gone home. Home to the solid brick ranch beside the cornfield. A stillness inside, as her family sits together in the living room, listening to the storm. Grateful for their lightning rod and foundation. As I pass the wing stand, I hear Bob practicing his chord progressions. "Goddamn it all," he says. "Damn it to hell."

Kathy is waiting for me in the bus. She's got the news on the big wall-mounted TV, sound down low, and has a strained look on her face. When I duck inside, the weatherman is pointing to a red pixilated mass that is moving in fits and starts across a map of the state. She looks up at me and re-arranges her face into a smile. "Just a summer storm," she says, reaching up to touch her earrings. "Nothing to worry about." She sounds as if she's trying to convince herself. Clicking off the TV, she pats the space beside her on the couch. "Look at you," she says, her voice changing when I don't sit. "Rough."

I walk back to the bedroom and lie down on the water bed without taking off my muddy boots. I hear her get up and start to make coffee. The rain comes in waves on the roof. It sounds like a hell of a lot more than a summer storm. It sounds like a wrathful sea.

"You're not sleeping in that truck tonight, Cole, baby," she calls back, running the water, opening the cupboards, banging around. It all sounds so forcedly cheerful that my mood goes dark like a burnt-out bulb.

"Got any other ideas?" I say to the wall. "Think Bob will mind if I shack up here?"

She's quiet, then says, "You could get a hotel."

The thought of driving into Thunderbird in the rain, past all those lighted houses, navigating the inevitable strip, finding the chain motel with its Shriners candy machines in the lobby and brochure rack of local attractions—it leaves me with a black hole of loneliness deep in my center.

"Cap's tight," I say, probably too quiet for her to hear. "There's worse things."

She comes in with two mugs of coffee, her rings clinking against them, squeezing sideways through the narrow door. She sits on the edge of the bed, sending a little wake rolling under me. A water bed in a bus, of all the things. She says she likes it, sleeping while Bob is driving, the little currents comforting, like the womb.

I know there's a part of Kathy that believes this bus will keep her young. That if she and Bob only keep moving, the odometer will spin on it, not her. As little kids, Clay and I thought that if you could just manage to keep your feet off the ground long enough, the world would revolve underneath you, and you'd come down in a different place than you left. We would take turns with a ruler, jumping as high as we could. Later we were fascinated with our grade school textbook's explanation of the speed of light. A story of twin brothers. One travels in a spaceship to distant galaxies and returns to find that while he has not aged at all, his brother is an old, old man. There was a cartoon illustration of the two of them face to face, an exclamation point in the air between them, the one who stayed behind with a beard like Rip Van Winkle. Clay and I discussed these things often, up past our bedtime, whispering in the darkness of his room. Atomic forces, galactic maps, the theory of relativity. His voice electric with excitement, my mind tripping over itself, trying to keep up with his.

I reach into my back pocket. "Present," I say.

Kathy gingerly takes the necklace from me and holds it between her fingertips. She turns it over and over, her lips tight. "Where'd you get this?" she finally says.

"Doesn't matter," I say, and cross my arms behind my head, feeling suddenly expansive. "It's for you."

She looks at me, one thin eyebrow raised, then slides a painted fingernail along the edge of the heart. It springs open like a door. Inside, there's a tiny picture of a baby, a red-faced newborn in a blue cap with a pinched, wrinkled face. We both look down at it, silent. The picture is small, no bigger than my pinky nail, but it suddenly feels as if there are three of us on the bus.

Snapping it shut, she hands it silently back. I take it, avoiding her eyes, and shove it deep in my pocket, as deep as it will go, wishing that it would disappear. I close my eyes and see the girl's grip on the bleachers, imagine the necklace swinging with each of his thrusts until it fell to the ground. A baby. It could be anyone, of course. A nephew, a cousin, an old picture of her brother, the one gone off to war. There is something tragic about it, the picture. But maybe it's just that look that newborns have, when it's hard to tell if they're alive or dead. I can feel Kathy watching me, waiting.

"You know that's someone's treasure," she finally says.

I keep my eyes shut and nod. Or the baby might be hers. No hope, then, of escape. Parked him with her mother the weekend of the fair so she can pretend for a day or two that she's free.

"I don't get you, Cole. What are you doing here? You've got your whole life ahead of you. You should make a home for yourself. Settle down."

"I like the road," I say, opening my eyes. Looking up at the close ceiling, the faux-marble panels and light fixtures, the words ring as hollow in the bus as they do inside my head.

She sighs. "But don't you ever think about the future?"

"I don't think about next week."

"Well, you live your life like that, Cole, baby, and one morning you'll wake up and it will have passed you by. Like that," she says, and snaps her fingers. "Believe me." I shift and look up at her hovering above me, her eyes sad and heavy. A sudden rush of rain pounds the roof, and a worried look passes over her face. No matter how far or how fast she travels, Kathy will grow old. She *is* old. I can see the wrinkles breaking through her thick makeup, the gray hair in her braids. The sagging flesh under her arms, gravity's toll.

She leans over as if to kiss me, but instead tries to fluff the pillow behind my head. In the penumbra of her smell, warm and soapy, I'm pushed down through fathomless depths, weighted with lead. The bed sloshes underneath me. The narrow walls of the bus are close and final as a casket. I jerk my head away from her and swing my feet onto the floor. The rain falls with the sound of tearing pages. In the lulls I can hear Bob's uncertain chords, his curses and false starts. I stand up on shaky legs, sick to death of other people's tragedies. To be carried away by a giant bird. There could be worse things. Everything and everyone on earth growing smaller and smaller, as all of it fell away.

"I've got to get out of here," I say.

Kathy sits up and slides her hands between her knees, trying to smile, to smooth it over. "Baby," she says, reaching out, and I step away, knocking into the flimsy closet door and sending a cascade of clothes out onto the floor. The rain roars on the roof. "Where on earth do you think you're going?"

·   ·   ·

The wind rips the door of the bus out of my hand as I dive out into the pounding rain. Pulling the collar of my shirt up around my neck, I duck my head and run down the empty path. Shouts and the beeps of backing trucks on the midway pierce the thick sound of the torrent. But none of it has been broken down yet—the rides are still up, the Ferris wheel looming above the crouching booths and trailers. Along the strips, figures in raincoats load pickups and tires spin in the mud. I run away from it all, out towards the dark field. The wet grass grabs at my legs, slowing me down, but I keep running until I'm at the tree line, and then I turn and look at the carnival, a somber city in the distance. When I pull the necklace from my pocket and let go, I expect it to be carried away on the wind. Instead it drops to the ground like an anchor, and I have to grind it into the mud with my boot to be rid of it. I want it never to be found again. Buried. Lost for good.

I'm the one who stayed. The brother with the beard. Clay reached escape velocity fifteen years ago, when he crashed his car that night, out on the dark road. I'm starting to think he was the lucky one. I stop and lean down on my knees, try to catch my breath, let the rain hammer me. The rain-swept field is desolate as the open sea. Virginia. Even if I was to turn around, drive east a thousand miles, pull onto the old road and down our driveway, I'd walk up a front path that leads to nothing, the house torn down months ago to make room for the new neighborhood that is rising up in the pasture where we spent our afternoons. Just Clay, me, and the old oak trees. And now the trees are gone, too.

"This is Illinois," I say, to steady myself. "My feet are on the ground." I crouch there, repeating it, until the rain stops. It stops abruptly, as if I have somehow willed it to, and in its place comes a thick, strange stillness, as if the palm of a giant hand has flattened over the field. Everything stands still— the grass, the leaves, the sky. I stand and look up, the towering dark clouds frozen. Clay had another favorite theory. If you could go up in a plane and travel around the equator at one thousand miles an hour, the speed of the earth's rotation there, the sun would appear to hang still in the sky. No past, no future. As long as you could keep up your speed.

"But," he'd say, frowning. "But there's a rub." It would be an illusion. Down on earth, the sun would be rising and setting, the clocks ticking away. Life would carry on without you.

Headlights come at me across the field. It's a cop car, bumping and straining over the uneven ground. The window rolls down as it pulls alongside me. Without stopping, a bull-faced sheriff leans out into the still air and jerks his thumb up towards the road, mistaking me for a straggling reveler. "Son," he says. "We've got a tornado warning in effect. We've sent everybody home."

Let it come, I think, running back up to the midway. Let it rip through. Let it wipe the field clean. Let it carry all this away. Up on my strip, my table stands alone, the tarp blown off my boxes, everything soaked. Dub's tent is gone, the only thing left an overturned folding chair. I can see a steady line of rigs leaving Camper City, pulling out onto the road, headed for God-knows-where. The rain starts again, all at once, pounding, and then the wind, picking it up and slashing it around. What I said to Kathy, about liking the road. That was a lie. The road—what it really is—eight lanes of grinding semis barreling west with spent uranium, east with old-growth timber, hauling shit-caked cows and microwave dinners, feeding the mad frenzy of this country—it all moves too fast. I've been thinking we'll just spin off our axis and out into the center of space. Hell, Thunderbird, Illinois, might be the first to go.

I run up the deserted paths of the midway, where rides and booths have been forsaken, left to the mercy of the wind. Flat-beds sit parked at abrupt angles next to the rides, some of which are partly dismantled, some still standing, the wind whistling through scaffolding. Paper plates, cups, and gnawed drumsticks spill out of overturned trash cans. A balloon caught on the side of the Haunted House beats itself against the wall, as if trying to break free. A loosed tarp swoops towards me on furious wings. I duck and it flings itself on down the path. I run past the Ferris wheel, where the plywood clown that kids must be as tall as to ride has toppled over and lies sideways, grinning, in the grass. The wheel shudders and groans. The carriages rock and glow in a flash of lightning. The wind shoves me along from behind.

My heart takes over, pounding, shouting from my chest. *Get out of here*, it shouts when I look up at the swaying wheel. *Get out of here*, it shouts, and the moaning steel struts of the Gravitron and Tilt-a-Whirl and Zipper all shout it too. Stumbling, I run through the rain towards the remains of Camper City, no idea what I'll do when I get there. Pull out on the road and try to outrun it, or lock the doors and watch it come. Either way, I've got nowhere to go.

But then I round the back loop, and see them. A ragged pack of boys, weaving through the abandoned booths. They're passing beer cans, trying to light cigarettes in the whipping wind. They must have hid when the cops came through, first brave, then reckless, defying the lightning. Now they're swaggering through the rain, invincible. And ahead of me, up on the carousel, girls in wet T-shirts sit astride the still horses, passing a bottle in a wet paper bag. The horses' nostrils flare, eyes and manes wild, legs flung out, suspended in mid-flight. Behind them, all of the sky is gathering itself up at the horizon, bloodred, feathered. The wind seems to hover above us. "Look!" I yell, pointing, but my voice is snatched away by the wind. The Ferris wheel groans, lamenting. "Get out of here! Go on!" But none of them even notice me. The girls cackle, their hair plastered to their faces, their eyes black with smudged makeup. The boys strut over, swing themselves up onto the horses, and shake the rain from their hair. They're all laughing, shouting, singing, celebrating as if they know something no one else knows. As if on the other side of that terrible horizon there's a new world coming when this one goes, a world where everything lost will be restored, and everything made whole. One of the girls, dark-eyed and wasted, sees me and reaches out, saying something I can't hear over the din, and I strain to make out her lips.

"Come on," she's saying, "come quickly, come, come—"

Reasons for and
Advantages of Breathing

Shell

I meet the herpetologist on the bus. Rush hour is in its deepest throes, a snowstorm has clamped down on the city, and the bus is packed with people in bulky coats, impatient and aggressive at the end of the day. Trapped at the center of the crush, I am starting to doubt that I will be able to hold it together all the way to my stop. Then a surge from behind sends me sliding into the man in front of me, and the flaps of a cardboard box he is holding pop open. I find myself looking down at a turtle, its shell mapped with orange and yellow and green. *A turtle!* I say as he gently folds the flaps back down. Then, shocked to hear myself unlock a door to conversation,

Do you mind if I see it again? He opens the box just enough for me to see inside. *Are you particularly interested in reptiles?* he says kindly. *Absolutely,* I say, though it isn't true. I just want to keep looking at the turtle, which has drawn its head inside its shell, so utterly still and complacent in the midst of the chaos of the bus. *It's rare to meet young people with an interest,* he says. *Oh, yes,* I say quickly, thrilled to be considered young. Then I look up at his face and realize how old he must be himself—gray beard, eyes big and watery behind thick glasses. *I'm a professor,* he says, *at the university. I've written a book you might find interesting.* He pulls a card from his pocket and points to the address with a shaky finger. *Drop by any time.*

Classification

Most nights, I don't sleep. Instead I lie in bed and page through my list of dread and regret, starting with my childhood and ending with the polar ice caps. Everything in between I file into something like schoolroom cubbies, marked with labels like DISASTER and DESIRE. When my husband left, he told me he hadn't been happy in years. *Happy?* I thought. *We're supposed to be happy?* I was under the impression that no one was truly happy, given the raw materials we have to work with in this life. Since he's been gone, I keep the lamp on all night. I'd rather lie awake in the light and keep an eye on his absence than reach out in the dark, thinking he's there. The fact that I may do this for the rest of my life is unclassifiable, too much to bear. When the list comes to this I get up and sit at the kitchen table and watch the snow, the snow that seems always to be falling.

Navigation

After looming for weeks, the day of my office Christmas party arrives. Every year it is the same. We all bring our husbands and wives to a third-rate steak house and get drunk and have a gift swap. The husbands and wives stand around making awkward small talk, and we all compliment one another on how nice we look out of our office clothes, drinking swiftly and heavily, sick to death of one another. At the center of all this sits an enormous, blood-rare roast. Last year my husband stole a bottle of vodka off the bar and we snuck out to the back alley, where we wrapped up in his coat and tried to name the constellations we could see between rooftops. The thing I was most grateful for: he could look at any situation, no matter how dire, and instantly know the best way to navigate through. If I was lucky, I'd be pulled along with him. At five o'clock someone comes by my cubicle and reminds me brightly, for the third time today, about the gift swap. I can see those gifts—the scented candles, the plush toys in Santa hats—already tossed in the garbage and on their way to the landfill. I reach into my bag for an aspirin and find the herpetologist's card. *I just remembered,* I say to no one in particular. *I have plans this afternoon.* I pull on my coat and hat and go, stumbling through the exhaust-stained snow, the wind slicing through my clothes. The university looms on a distant hill. When I finally arrive, it seems deserted, nothing but an expanse of iced-over parking lots. It takes a while to find the building whose name is printed on the herpetologist's card, and just as I am about to give up I see it, a low industrial structure that sits on the edge of the campus like an afterthought. Inside, the halls are ill-lit and empty. I follow the signs to the herpetology department. Down one flight of stairs, then another, then another. With each flight I grow warmer, strip off a layer—coat, hat, sweater, scarf. By the time I have found the herpetologist's office, deep in the basement, I am breathless and damp with sweat.

Anticipation

When I knock, the herpetologist flings open his door and beams at me, ushering me in. The tiny room is tropically warm, one wall lined with aquariums that glow with ultraviolet light. *This is my office,* he says proudly, *and those are my anoles.* He is wearing battered khakis and sandals with socks, as if he has just come from a jungle expedition. The anoles give the room a frantic energy. They puff and posture, do push-ups, circle one another warily. Their bodies are sharp and lizard-like, the dulled green and brown of sea glass, and fans of brightly colored skin hang from their chins: red, purple, blue. *Do you want to hold one?* the herpetologist asks, eyes sparkling. When I step closer, their faces seem wise and irascible, and as they swivel their eyes I get the sense that they are sizing me up. But the herpetologist has already pulled the mesh cover off one of the tanks and is watching me, expectant. I reach in and make a halfhearted show of trying to catch one, my hand sending streaks of panic through the tank. I look at him and shrug. *Like this,* he says, and I see his hand slip in like a stealthy animal. Suddenly, an anole is clasped in his fingers, its head between his thumb and forefinger, tongue flickering, as startling as a bright scarf conjured in a magic trick. I gasp, my lungs blooming with the warm air, and find I've been holding my breath. *You've got to anticipate,* he says, grinning.

Raft

I come home to a red light flashing in the dark of the living room: a message on the machine from my husband. I have to play it twice—his voice is slurred and halting. This is how it has been for several months: when he gets drunk, he wants to work it out. I call him back and tell him to come over, willing to take him any way I can get him. He arrives already bristling with defenses, a cape of snow on his shoulders. As we stand there in the living room, hashing it all out, I try to keep it together by fixing my eyes on the snow, watching the flakes turn to drops of water and then disappear into the fabric of his coat. A brand-new coat, I notice, and I am sideswiped by an image of his new apartment, where I've never been, all the furniture I know he has treated himself to—top of the line, paid on credit, same-day delivery, as if he can buy his way back to a beginning. Exhausted, I collapse into him, and he pilots me towards the bed, but when we make love I feel as if I am struggling for a grip on a slippery raft, trying in vain to pull myself up. Afterwards, we are lying side by side, not touching, when he turns to me and flexes the mattress with his fingers. *I know why you can't sleep,* he says. *It's obvious. What you need are individually wrapped coils.* When he falls asleep I turn on the light and watch his eyes flutter in a dream. I imagine all his women, in there with him. I close my eyes and picture them, one by one, lingering on the torturous details: their optimism, their young skin, their white teeth flashing as they smile at him across his expensive new bed. But in between, I find I keep seeing the herpetologist's office. Familiar, like an ill-used back room of my mind: the glow of the lamps, the dust-cloaked bookshelves, the anoles—a many-colored bouquet.

Adaptation

On the coldest day of December, the heat goes out at work. I sit hunched at my desk, freezing, my hands pulled up into my sleeves, dreaming about the tropical warmth of the lamps in the herpetologist's office. I get up, switch off the computer, and go. Outside, a thick sleet is falling, turning the city the color of asphalt. The cold air slices through my clothes. When I arrive I try to think up a reason for why I've returned, but the herpetologist takes my coat without question and in fact seems overjoyed to see me. *Let me show you the lab,* he says, clasping my arm. *Is it as warm as your office?* I ask sheepishly. *Warmer!* he says. *Come on.* Our shoes squeak on the linoleum as we walk down the long hall. No one else seems to be around. He opens the door of the lab with a key on his crowded ring. At first, the room seems full of empty aquariums. Then, slowly, as the herpetologist leads me from one to the next, the animals reveal themselves. There is a sidewinder and a hellbender. There is a chuckwalla from Texas that, when it sees us, rushes between two rocks in its habitat and puffs itself up until it is wedged tightly in. There is a nightmarish creature from Australia called a thorny devil, with spines that have spines. Its Latin name, typed on a card taped to its aquarium, is *Moloch horridus.* In the next cage, a giant Gila monster sleeps under a heat lamp, its sides pooled out around it, POISONOUS! written in red on its card. A brilliant green gecko uses its tongue to wipe its eyes. The herpetologist's face is shining. *All these diverse adaptations, with one common goal,* he says. *To live to see tomorrow.* He turns abruptly towards the back of the room, tripping over a cardboard box full of crickets. *Come here,* he says, motioning, and I go to him and watch a barking tree frog, an impossible, unnatural yellow, delicately eat a fly out of his hand.

Natural History

My husband and I sit side by side on the couch in the light of one lamp. We say the same things we always do, slicing back through the scar tissue in one another's heart. *I've always felt,* he says, *that you never had any hope for us.* I stare at the puddle of melted snow around his boots by the front door, no idea where to begin. My hopelessness extends to include the entire human race. We've mortgaged our lives, ruined the planet, and with modern technology rendered ourselves nearly obsolete. What is there to hope for? Who is equipped to take on what's to come? I saw our love as a fallout shelter for the future, and thought he did too. But all along he'd been with other women, with whom, he told me, he could have fun. *Fun*. When we make love I stare up at the ceiling, already imagining him pulling his pants back on, sliding into those boots, sneaking out soundlessly in the morning while I squeeze my eyes shut, feigning sleep.

Night Vision

I come home the next evening to find a dark snake draped across the foot of the bed. Motionless, waiting for my next move. I freeze, thrilled to the sheer shock of it. My pulse rips with terror and delight. Fingers quivering, I switch on the light. But it is only my husband's limp black sock, left from last night. Caught where it landed when we pulled off our clothes once words had failed us, as they always have.

Spadefoot Toad

Walking home from work, I go far out of my way to pass the university. I descend the steps to the herpetologist's office with as much sense of purpose as if I have been given my own key. He is at his desk when I arrive, and he looks up from his papers and tells me about the spadefoot toad. *You're lucky to see one in the wild,* he says. *They burrow deep, deep in the ground. They've been found, unharmed, among the embers of brushfires. And,* he says, dropping his voice, leaning in close, *they freeze solid in winter. Solid. Like an ice cube. You could actually pick one up and throw it against a wall, and it would shatter.* As he says this, he makes the motion one would make to dash a frog against a wall, as if sidearming a tennis ball. His glasses slip off with the effort, and he fumbles for them with both hands. The silence that follows is intimate and close. Startled by this, I search his face, wondering if he notices it too. His gray beard is etched in red, annals of his younger self. Suddenly I want to tell him everything, things I have been afraid even to tell my husband. *I tried to kill myself once,* I say. *When I was young. I jumped off a bridge into a half-frozen river.* The herpetologist is quiet for so long that I wonder if I shouldn't have said it, then wish I could take it back. Finally he says, *And were you shivering, when they pulled you out? Of course I was shivering,* I say, confused. He nods. *Trust the body, not the mind,* he says, smiling. *The body loves itself.*

Habitat

On Christmas Eve, I end up at another party. Every instinct says not to go, but it's no time to be alone, I keep telling myself, and there's a possibility my husband may be there. I manage to get myself into a dress and a pair of panty hose and go. By the time I arrive, tight packs of people are already impenetrably formed around the room, plates expertly balanced, voices tinkling. I find a drink and arrange myself near the hors d'oeuvres, where I keep an eye on the door and stab my drink with its tiny straw. As time wears on, my panty hose sag around my thighs, hobbling me there. I watch the faces around the room, wondering how everyone can be having such a good time, given the devastating stories I'm sure that they too all saw on the six o'clock news. The only thing keeping me going is the Christmas tree, which smells like bracing outdoor work, well-being, and fulfillment. The hostess comes over and offers me another drink. *The tree smells lovely,* I say, motioning to it across the room. *Oh!* she says gaily. *It's a spray!* and sweeps away to fill my drink. I carry myself like a broken glass to the dark of the corner, where at least I can yank up my sagging panty hose. Sliding behind the tree, I see the holes in the plastic trunk where the wire branches screw in. A new low, to be failed by a tree. I grasp a bough between my thumb and forefinger for balance and find that I am nonetheless searching its needles for any sign of life, hoping for anything, the blink of an eye, a flash of a disappearing tail.

A Gift

On Christmas morning I step out onto the stoop and find the herpetologist's book, laid carefully on a patch of white ice. A bright green chameleon is staring up at me from the dust jacket, its eye following my every move. When I pick it up I open to a mimeographed list of errata pasted to the flyleaf. The copyright date is thirty years ago. I turn to the back flap, hoping to see a photograph of the herpetologist as a young man, but there is only a list of his degrees and credentials. On the inside front cover, there is an inscription made out to me: *With warmest regards.* Only then do I wonder how he found my apartment. I stay home all day and read it cover to cover. I read that, at six weeks, a human embryo is nearly identical to a salamander's—gill slits, webbed hands, tail bud. I read that snakes have two hundred pairs of ribs and tiny, vestigial leg bones. I read all about hibernation and estivation. In the section on evolution, I find a chapter titled "Reasons for and Advantages of Breathing."

Perpetuation

A bullfrog in a corner aquarium has laid her eggs. They float in a raft of jelly on the surface of the water, knocking against the glass. The big green frog courses around, kicking her thick thighs, oblivious to them. *In the wild, she'd be long gone by now,* the herpetologist says. *Her existence is a perpetual struggle. She can't be burdened by babies. But still, she must replace herself.* I think of all of us, people racing around trying to leave something to the world as we put the world itself at stake in the process. *What's the point?* I don't realize I've said it aloud. *Who knows?* the herpetologist says. He taps the glass. *Ask her.* I turn towards him. *Did you ever have children?* He shakes his head. *Always been married to my work. We never did,* I say. *My husband wanted to. But I just couldn't bring a child into this world. I don't know. Do you think I should have?* He shakes his head. *Should have, should have,* he says. *Look at her.* He taps the glass again. *She knows no such word as "should." She knows only "can" and "do."* I look down at the eggs. There must be thousands of them, each with a dark spot at the center like the pupil of an eye, and I am suddenly dismayed by the thought of the mother kicking away from them without leaving behind so much as a promise. *How many will make it?* I ask. The herpetologist ticks off the hazards that would face the eggs in the wild: flood, drought, pollution, construction, snakes, fish, turtles, toads, raccoons, other frogs. *The tadpole stage is even chancier,* he says, *and you can just about forget it when you're a froglet.* Then he says, *But at least one.* One? I think, looking at the mass of eggs with a sinking sense of despair. Which one? The lucky one?

Locomotion

On a day with little else to justify my getting out of bed in the morning, the herpetologist gives me a turtle skeleton. *A turtle's backbone is fused to its carapace,* he chants, *an arching armature for its armor.* The neck and leg bones are impossibly frail, fine as pebbles. They seem far too delicate to support the heavy awning of the shell. *Yes,* the herpetologist says, seeing me looking, *poorly designed for locomotion on land. No lateral possibility, with those bones.* He takes the skeleton from me and shows me how a turtle moves: lifting two legs, deliberately throwing itself off balance until it falls forward. Lifting the other two legs and falling forward again. Falling, picking itself up, falling. *Like this, the turtle has lurched its way through two hundred million years. Through all kinds of weather.* This strikes me as the most remarkable thing I've heard in months. *Humbling,* I say. *Yes! But think of your own skeleton,* he tells me. *The bipedal frame is a triumph of design. Thirty-three articulated vertebrae, all in a line. And at the tip, the unparalleled mass of electricity that is your mind. And you didn't even have to ask for it.*

Range

As I walk through the frozen city, I do think of it, my skeleton hanging in perfect balance. The bones of my toes and feet, flexing inside my shoes. I trace them up my shinbones, the long bones of my thighs, up the ladder of my spine. All the way up to the thought that I could walk for miles, hundreds of miles if I so chose, clear out of the city to a warmer place.

Company

On New Year's Eve I go out for a walk, surprised by a sudden desire to breathe the sharp night air. People scurry through the street two by two, heads bent against the cold, wearing their best clothes. The men check their watches as if there is a train to catch, headed for a fabulous destination. A man and a woman are leaning close to a shop window, their voices filled with delight. It is my husband with a much younger woman, both dressed for a party. When he looks up and sees me, a strangled noise escapes his throat. *I don't want to see you anymore,* I say, because it's all I've got. *Okay,* he says, *all right,* not even pretending to put up a fight. As they walk away and join the throng on the street, I get the sense that the train is departing imminently, and that there's no chance that I will be on it. I look in the window at what they had been examining. It is a glittering diamond and emerald brooch, something I myself have admired in the past. But now it seems gaudy and crude, and I realize I was expecting something infinitely more beguiling to be crouched behind the glass. I hear a noise behind me and wheel around, thinking that maybe he's come back, but it is just a lone crow, picking delicately through an overturned trash can. It feels as if we're the last two creatures left in the abandoned city, just me and this crow. Grateful for the company, I raise my hand. *Oh, hello,* I say.

Las Vegas Leopard Frog

There is a grainy black-and-white photograph of a frog taped above the herpetologist's desk. It is an ordinary-looking frog. Beneath the photo hangs a narrow page torn from a field guide. I read it so many times I am able to repeat it from memory, or almost. It reassembles itself in my mind as a sort of a poem:

Last seen in 1942, long before worry about endangered
  species
Probably extinct
As the city of Las Vegas grew
groundwater pumped out,
springs capped
hope for *Rana fisheri* was filled in with cement
Discovery of a remnant population
would be a herpetological event

Deficiency

The herpetologist needs my help. *I wouldn't ask,* he says on
the phone, *except that no one else is here.* A snake has just been
brought in, a confiscated reticulated python that someone
has been keeping as a pet. When I arrive, the herpetologist
is standing in front of its tank, dwarfed by it. *I'm afraid it
must be destroyed,* he tells me sadly. *It has an irreversible and
degenerative vitamin deficiency, resulting from an inadequate
diet. Nothing can be done.* I watch it slowly map the terrain of
its tank, staggered with disbelief that someone would keep
such a massive, commanding thing in the house and not take
pains to see that it has everything it needs. *Ready to shed,
too,* the herpetologist says, pointing to its milk-white eyes.
*Dull all over. Would be brilliant in a week or two. I've seen them
tie themselves in knots in an effort to shed the old skin. What a
shame,* I say, and feel a shiver of grief as the loss suddenly

multiplies—the snake, and the newness the snake won't have the chance to inhabit. *People,* the herpetologist sighs. I help him hold the snake as he makes the injection, and in my hands I feel a change in the taut muscles, the exact moment that life leaves them. We hold vigil over the enormous body. The herpetologist looks stricken, drawn and old. *I don't know,* he says over and over. *I just don't know.* I shove my hands in my pockets, wishing I could give him something. We stand there together for a long time, bewildered as two night travelers with a map they can't make out in the dark.

Bloom

All night, I lie awake in the light of the bedside lamp, studying my hands. What was it, exactly, that I felt pass out of the snake? The one thing I know for certain: I've witnessed a slight parting of the curtain that hangs over the unknown. By morning I feel a bloom of gratitude for this, which I wear, a bright badge, pinned to my chest for days.

Heralds of Spring

I leave my apartment at five to help the herpetologist with his morning feedings. So this is what it feels like, I think, to be out at dawn, meeting the world head on. Salt trucks are rumbling by, preparing the icy streets for the coming day. The sky is a color I've never seen before. It is as if a corner of the city's gray overcoat has blown back to reveal an orange satin lining.

We drink Postum out of Styrofoam cups. He apologizes that there is no real coffee. I tell him I don't drink it anymore, a last attempt to reclaim sleep. *Good girl,* he says, *good girl.* He pulls a record off the bookshelf and puts it on the turntable. Through the scratchiness I hear a high-pitched, insistent whistle, like crickets, only the notes are rounder, wetter, like water dropping from a leaf into a pond. *The dawn song of the peeper,* he says, *the herald of spring.* He beams. *I don't think spring is ever coming,* I say. *Nonsense,* he says. *And in a week or so, the students will come back. I must say, as much as I enjoy the quiet, it does get lonely around here when they're gone.* The students! The fact of them has never occurred to me. Now I see their bright, eager faces, I see them shaking snow off their boots and talking excitedly, listening raptly to the herpetologist in a lecture room, notebooks open, carrying him away in a wave down the hall. The record switches to the call of a bullfrog, mournful. I have the sudden urge to reach behind me and lock the door.

Secret

I want you to see something, the herpetologist says. *A secret.* He leads me to a door at the back of the lab that I haven't noticed before. He selects a large key from his ring and unlocks it. We step into a tiny antechamber, and when he closes the door behind us, we stand together for a moment in the utter darkness. Then I hear the click of a key in another lock, and we step through to another room, even darker than the first. He switches on a dim red light. As my eyes adjust I see a chest-high tank of water in the center of the room. We step to its edge. In the red light I can just make out something swimming around in the water, tiny ghost creatures with red ruffs of gills. *The Georgia blind salamander,* he whispers. *It exists only in the deep wells and subterranean waters of one particular farm in southeast Georgia. You're maybe the tenth person in the world to see one alive.* The salamanders seem to give off a light of their own, dark eye buds showing through the clear skin of their faces, their red gills waving like feathers as they weave through the water. For a heartbeat I forget myself completely. Then I catch my breath and say, *They don't even know we're here.* The herpetologist moves closer. I slip my hand in his. *I think I love you,* I say. He shakes his head firmly, as if it's the wrong answer to a question. *No, you don't.*

A Herpetological Event

I stay late at work, in no state to face my dark apartment, overcome by a new sort of loneliness, one that seems as if it will outlive me. By the time I get on the bus, late in the evening, it is hushed and mostly empty, and I collapse into a seat near the back. As we rattle down the street I close my eyes and think of the blind salamanders, down there in their well in Georgia, far from the city, far from me. When I open my eyes I have long since missed my stop. I sit up in a panic, recognizing nothing outside. But then, as the bus voyages through unfamiliar streets, the salamanders come back like a dream.

The darkness deep in the earth where they've been all along. Arcing, looping, somersaulting through the water, somehow finding one another in the dark. Without any thought, care, or need for me. And for a instant, just before the bus turns on its loop, I catch a glimpse of the infinite. There I am inside of it, for one suspended moment—tiny, inconsequential, and utterly free.

Dawn Song

Late in the night a storm settles on the city, throwing snow against the windows and rattling them in their frames. My husband calls to tell me his power has gone out and asks if he can come over. *Just this one night,* he says. *I don't have anywhere else to go.* I sit at the kitchen table waiting for him, listening to the silence of the streets, the weather too bad for even the plows to be out. Things are so still that I am startled to look down and see the collar of my robe is quivering steadily with my pulse. He comes in with a red wind-burned face and cold clinging to his clothes. We sit side by side at the table, no words left for one another. Soon my power goes out as well and there is nothing for us to do but get into bed and huddle beneath the blankets, press tight together to conserve warmth. We make love, a matter of survival, our bodies desperate to generate heat. My heart pounds against his chest with the insistence of self-preservation, tenacious and bright. It is still beating hard, determined, by the time he has fallen asleep. I sit up and try to make out his sleeping face in the dark, left with the unshakable feeling that there is a stranger in my bed. Sometime before dawn I get up in the cold room to look out the window. The snow is slackening, but down the block, all the street lights are still off. In the darkness, the shine of the deep, white drifts is the only thing I can make out. It seems to conceal a great mystery, the snow. I stand there watching, struck by the possibility of what might be hidden beneath. I watch for as long as I can stand the cold, knowing that by morning the trucks will have come to clear it all away.

This Is Not a Love Story

It is a reckless venture, motherhood. I know you can't hang on to them forever, but it's downright crazy when you think about it: you take such good care of them—you trim their tiny fingernails so carefully when they are babies, you make sure they drink their milk and eat their vegetables and look both ways before crossing, you minister to every scrape and bruise, and then they turn eighteen—that's it—you just turn them out into the wilderness.

My daughter left home for college last week. I am still peering in the doorway of her room when I go by, thinking I will see her, cross-legged on the bed. The dog waits for her on the front porch all afternoon. An unnatural silence hangs over the house in the evening. Last night at dinner, my husband looked up at me and said, "So what do you plan to do with yourself, now that you have all this *time?*"

Time. When I was young, I thought I had all the time in the world. Time to waste. Time to make mistakes. It never crossed my mind that I might wake up one morning and it would be gone, just like that.

When she was packing, my daughter found a box of black-and-white photographs down in the basement. I hadn't seen them since before she was born. When she brought the box upstairs and spread them out on the kitchen table—my God—it was like she had dredged up a body, a missing life. Case long since closed.

What could I do? I told her the story. There it was, after all, laid out on the table: my one spectacularly wrong turn.

At the age of twenty-two, I somehow got it in my head that I would be a photographer. The next Stieglitz or Evans or Arbus. I do not have a creative bone in my body, but it was the artist's life I was drawn to, or what I thought an artist's life was about—beauty, spontaneity, freedom—everything my parents' life lacked. I came up with a plan to move to the South, where I had never been and which seemed so mysterious: raw and dangerous and full of relics of a long-gone era. This mystery, I truly believed, would more than make up for my lack of talent, because any photograph I took could not help but capture it.

If only someone had given it to me straight. If only someone had been kind enough to discourage me. My parents just threw up their hands and vowed not to give me a penny. But who needed money? I had higher pursuits. I packed up my car and drove until I got to Georgia, to a little town where, in 1984, they still had dirt roads and a crossroads jailhouse and a general store where old men sat around a checkerboard on a whiskey barrel, and down a dark hallway there were two bathrooms still marked with the faint, chilling outline of the words WHITE and COLORED.

I should have known right away that I was in over my head—should have got back in the car and driven straight home to Connecticut. Instead I rented a place, made a darkroom out of the closet, and got a job waiting tables at a dingy restaurant by a lake. The lake was one of those fake lakes they've got down there, where sometime in the 1940s the government built a dam on a river and flooded a whole town. You would never know it, to look at it. I assumed the lake was just like the lakes we have here in the north, formed perfectly naturally by the slow scrape of glaciers. But nothing was what it seemed to be, in Georgia. Nothing was what it seemed, nothing was permanent, and so much was concealed—a town under water, a rattlesnake den under a boulder—hazards that a girl like me wouldn't even know to look for.

Tommy came in to the restaurant all the time, but at first I did not notice him. He was twice my age, with a beard and a beer paunch, a leathery tan and mirrored sunglasses, just like all the other customers who came in for catfish and hush puppies or chicken-fried steak, all those dreadful things they served at that place, after a day of fishing on the lake. But Tommy wasn't a fisherman—he hated to see an animal suffer, any animal—and one day, I went to clear his table and found the tip he had left me: five one-dollar bills, folded to look like a tiny bouquet of roses. I was charmed.

Tommy, I would learn soon enough, was famous for tricks like that. Useless tricks, party tricks. He could strike a match on his front teeth and get the cap off a beer bottle in half a dozen different ways. He could speak Pig Latin and fold a napkin to look like a dancing chicken and eat fire if he was drunk enough. He could play a guitar behind his back. The kind of skills some men spend their twenties perfecting, but promptly lose to lack of practice when they get real jobs and families. Not Tommy. Tommy hadn't held down a real job in decades, and as for a family, though he'd been married once, briefly, when he was young, he had not had anyone steady in his life since. This should have been enough of a warning. Forty-five and still living life like he was eighteen.

He was staying on a houseboat docked at the marina—that should have been the next red light. The boat wasn't even his—it belonged to a friend who let Tommy crash out there when he was low on money, and he'd been there for over a year. There was Astroturf on the deck, and below there was a galley kitchen, a tiny cave of a bedroom, mold along the edges of the carpet, and beach chairs for furniture. A leaky fuel line made the living quarters dizzying with fumes. But the first night I went out there and we motored out to the middle of the lake to watch the moon rise, in silence save for the lapping of the water, the crickets on the far shore, and the ice popping and melting in our drinks, I looked up at the stars and curled my toes in my sandals and thought, *My God, why would anyone want to live on land?* I thought I had found it, the life I was looking for.

I remember the parties best. Oh, my, those were some parties. You would wake up in the morning and figure the earth had to have shifted on its axis. It is a wonder no one ever drowned, or burned their hands off—the fireworks! Every night like the Fourth of July. Roman candles lined up along the rail. When they sailed off hissing into the water, Tommy would smile contentedly and watch them like they held messages to be delivered to another world.

It was a real cast of characters at those parties—grizzled old bikers, Southern belles with big hair who drank like fish and cussed like sailors, a revolving pack of skinny teenage boys whose tan bodies are forever imprinted on my mind at the moment they would dive off the back, one after another, like a chorus line. How did Tommy assemble such a crew? Some of them were old friends or, like the bikers, had worked with Tommy on an odd job somewhere, but many he would have just met a day or two before: the sons and daughters of vacationing families from Atlanta whom he befriended at the gas station or the general store. And then there was me. I must have looked to all of them exactly like what I was: a wide-eyed Yankee college girl, clutching a camera to her chest, too shocked and shy to take pictures. You have got to be bolder, you know, to be behind a camera than to be in front of one.

And Tommy—Tommy would be in the middle of it all, holding court in an open Hawaiian shirt and train engineer's cap, a beer in each hand, putting them down only to light another firework or slide another tape in the stereo. You name it, he played it, and played it loud: that music must have carried over the water all the way down to Florida.

Then right in the middle of a song—he had the attention span of a four-year-old—all of a sudden he would snap off the stereo and pick up his fiddle. He could play any instrument that was handed to him, and play it beautifully—make you want to weep it was so beautiful, especially after what you'd been listening to all night. Old hymns, folk songs that he learned from his grandfather, who was, he'd never let you forget, the grandson of a Confederate captain. Even the titles made me teary. "There Will Be Peace in the Valley." "Come All Ye Fair and Tender Ladies." There was one—"Drunken Hiccups"—I must have heard him play that one a hundred times, but I never did know how it ended. He would pluck the fiddle strings to make it hiccup, and exaggerate his drawl. Everyone would sing along:

> *If the river was whiskey and I was a duck*
> *I'd dive to the bottom and drink my way up*
> *But the river ain't whiskey and I ain't a duck—*

They never got to the last line, because one of his buddies would stop there and shout, "It ain't a river, Tommy! It's a goddamn lake!" And another would jab a beer can in the air and yell back gleefully, "And it ain't whiskey! It's beer! It's cheap-ass beer!" And one of the boys would do a double gainer off the back, and Tommy would lean back in his lawn chair, pull me close with the bow, laugh, and kiss me. Oh, he was a charmer, that Tommy. And I fell for every last bit of it.

When people talk about the South being haunted, it's true. But it's not the places that are haunted, it's the people. They are trapped by all the stories of the past, wandering a long hallway lined with locked doors, knocking and knocking, with no one ever answering. No one ever will. That's the thing about the past. The closest you can get to it is stories, and stories don't even come close.

Everyone talked about the town at the bottom of the lake as if it was only yesterday they had been doing their grocery shopping there. Tommy could stand there all night, drinking beer and reminiscing. He was only a little boy when they built the dam, but he seemed to remember everything: the oak tree with a cannon ball from a Civil War skirmish still wedged in its trunk, the houses, the library, the hardware store. I would squint at the water and try to picture it—I never could.

The truth was that town was dead, all those old trees were dead, and the people were dead or had moved to Valdosta forty years before. All that was left was that big fake lake, with its choppy shoreline and muddy stink, the water skiers and mosquitoes big as hummingbirds, and the restaurant where I made terrible tips and the marina with numbered slips for thirty-five boats, and Tommy and me wrapped in each other's arms in slip number thirty-three, once the party had finally folded and everyone else had gone home.

.   .   .

Tommy gave me a dog that summer, a little black-and-white mutt he found abandoned in the marina parking lot and befriended with hot dogs and tuna fish. He really did want me to have it, but that dog was never mine. Never even gave me the time of day, but I didn't mind. It was something else, to watch that dog with Tommy. It was absolutely devoted to him, just glued to his hip. He taught it to shake and speak and dive with him off the side of the boat. They would both scramble up on deck, dripping wet and panting, great big grins on their faces, while I sat in the lawn chair and applauded. At night, the dog slept under the bed, as close to Tommy as we would allow. To use an expression of Tommy's, that dog thought he had hung the moon.

But every once in a while, something would come over that dog. Something would come over it, and it would not let Tommy near. It would be lying there, perfectly at peace, sound asleep in the sun on the top deck, and then Tommy would come up the ladder and it would leap to its feet, hackles raised, baring its teeth and growling like a hell-hound. Send him crawling right back down the ladder. Poor Tommy. That just tore him up. He couldn't understand. "That dog's just crazy," I would tell him, trying my best to comfort him. "Dr. Jekyll and Mr. Hyde. Don't pay any attention to it."

But the dog wasn't crazy—it was smart. I didn't realize it at the time, but that dog could see clear into Tommy— clear through to his heart—to both the good and the dark.

Tommy couldn't fool that dog the way he was fooling everybody else.

Oh, everyone knew he was drinking too much. *He* knew he was drinking too much. But he knew how far he could push it—and then just at the last moment, just when it seemed he had passed the point of no return, just when his bad side started to break through, the mood swings, the yelling—he knew how to reel it back in. And when that time came—I was a woman on a mission. Clearing out all the beer bottles, sniffing out the secret stash. The parties would go dry—yes, there was plenty of other stuff going on, but no one would have a drink for a week. Tommy would be as gentle as a kitten. Then one morning he'd roll over and look at me with those eyes. "Baby, can I have some money?" How could I refuse? He would drive off and come back with three cases of beer. And it would start all over again.

He had been through all the programs. He could talk the talk. "Sure, I'm on the twelve-step program," he would say. "At all times keep the beer cooler no farther than twelve steps away." When he was drinking, he could make you feel like you were in on it with him. That you were pulling the big one over on somebody. That's what Tommy was too damn good at. Making everybody feel like they were on his team. And what other team would you ever want to be on?

There was a running joke at those parties. "Denial," Tommy would say, cracking a beer with a theatrical sigh and shaking his head. The first time I heard it, I held my breath, thinking things had taken a bad turn. I looked around. Everyone else was frozen too, faces serious. But that was just part of the act. After a minute or two of that strained silence, someone would pipe up, "What are you talking about, Tommy? De river in Egypt?" And the crowd would explode.

But it wasn't a river anymore. Hadn't been for forty years. It was a lake, a goddamn lake, and on a lake you can't really go anywhere. On a lake the best you can hope for is around and around.

By Labor Day, I had forgotten that the North, or anything in it, even existed. Though it was just as hot as July, the lake quieted down beautifully; the vacationers left, the retirees abandoned their boats for the season, the water skiers packed it in, the restaurant served its last hush puppy, gave me my last paycheck, and shuttered its windows and doors.

Tommy would drive me all over the county so that I could shoot rolls of film. He would pull over when he saw something he thought would make a good picture—kids playing marbles in a yard, vultures in a kudzu-covered tree, a field of rusted cars—and shoo me out with my camera. I'd stand there fussing with my light meter, framing the shot, and double-checking everything, and Tommy would hang his sunburned elbow out the window and shout, "All right already! Just press the damn shutter!" Once in a while, he would grab the camera and take the picture himself, and later, when I printed it up, I would see how good it was. After a while—it's a shame—I got so jealous that I told him not to do it any-more. And he didn't.

Weeknights, Tommy and I had the lake to ourselves. For a while he wasn't drinking much at all. We were living on no money, which thrilled me. The evenings were warm. We would skinny dip at sunset and he would laugh at me, the way I pad-dled around with my neck craned, refusing to get my hair wet. The dog was devoted as ever, swimming joyous circles around us. We would discuss our children. I wanted six of them.

"Walter," I would say. "Margaret, Robert, Jane, Richard, Nancy."

"Bonaparte," he would say, arcing a mouthful of water at me. "Aloysius, Ruby Pearl, Brutus, Octavia, Percival."

"Tommy!" I'd say, splashing him. "Be serious."

He would pull me close under the water and kiss me. "I am being serious," he would grin.

Did things start to go bad because the parties stopped? Or did the parties stop because things started to get bad? I never have figured that out, and I guess it doesn't really make sense to try. By that point, I was a goner. I was just a moon in Tom-my's orbit, controlled by his gravity, chained to him. All I could do was look in his eyes in the morning and know what kind of go-round I was going to have that day.

That fall he started to disappear. Gone all day, sometimes all night. I knew it wasn't another woman—Tommy was noth-ing if not faithful. No—he was paying visits to all his ghosts. I could only guess where he went. And what did I know? When it came down to it, I didn't have the first clue about that place, or who Tommy had been before I came along, or what those ghosts might even look like.

Night after night, alone in that bed, it was like sleeping in a hospital waiting room. I'd wake up a dozen times with the same two thoughts whirling around in my head: *How much longer, and how bad is it?* And then at dawn I would hear his footsteps above me, the dog would come slinking out from under the bed, the motor would cough to a start, and by the time I got up on deck we'd be halfway out to the center of the lake, Tommy at the wheel with a cigarette hanging out of his mouth, and a look I knew better than to argue with.

It exhausts me to think about it, even now. Like trying to hold a drowning man's head above water. The nights I would drive to Valdosta, going in and out of bars, searching for him. Dragging him out, driving him home, arguments that he would not remember in the morning. The last few parties that turned ugly, blood on the deck. One night, I poured every can of beer and every bottle of liquor overboard. I didn't know what else to do. He pounded down the dock, raging. I heard the slam of his truck door echo in the empty parking lot. Heard him tear out. Let the last bottle *glug glug* into the water. *But the river ain't whiskey and I ain't a duck—*

The trouble was, I knew exactly what I wasn't. I just didn't know who I *was*.

I huddled up in bed, and waited.

Ice formed on the edges of the puddles in the parking lot.

The dog, permanently spooked, up and ran away for good.

When Tommy smashed up my camera one night, I did not even care. I had forgotten all about it. For the best, anyway. If one thing was certain, I never had what it took to be a photographer.

"That's not true," my daughter said. She pushed her chair back from the kitchen table, where she had been studying the photographs, and held up two of them. "These two are really good. These two are great."

I looked at them. They were. They were Tommy's.

I have never liked the expression, *He drank himself to death.* It makes it sound as if someone sits down with that purpose in mind, rather than it being something that just happens along the way. I don't know what became of Tommy. When I got out I didn't look back. But those are precisely the words that come to mind every time I allow myself to wonder about him.

And if he did? Well, if he did, I wasn't going to save him. No, I wasn't going to save him, just the same as I wasn't going to find anyone else like him, despite the years I spent—the years I wasted—trying.

My daughter put down the photographs and looked at me. So beautiful. That clear face. Her father's eyes.

"God, Mom," she said. "It sounds like those were the days."

No, I told her.

"But wasn't it worth it?" she said. "Wouldn't you do it all over again?"

No, it wasn't worth it, I told her. Not any of it.

Not one damn minute of it.

Trust me.

Kidding Season

Charlie was headed to the Gulf. Since the hurricane, he had heard, the jobs were there for the taking. The kid who pumped gas at the Shell back in Red Bank had been down for a week in March and told him all about it. Places were cheap, the water was warm, and the girls were looking for action. "Good thing for Category Five hurricanes," he said, and it struck Charlie that this was a hateful thing to say just as he realized it was exactly where he needed to go.

Lucy's farm was only a stopover, a place to hide out, save up some money, and then get back on the road. Goats, Charlie figured. How much work could they really be? Getting out of Red Bank—that had been the hard part.

He was wrong, it turned out, on both counts. The days at Lucy's felt like a broken record, a never-ending limbo. He just couldn't seem to get anything right. Not to mention the weather, which looked like it was there to stay. Triple digits for a week, hot as the hinges of hell, and going on forty-five days with no rain.

People were saying it was the worst drought in a century. Charlie, wrestling with the crazy-wheeled wheelbarrow, already sweating at seven-thirty in the morning, figured it had to be the worst drought in a million years. The pastures were as scorched as a space shuttle launch site. The low hills in the distance sizzled in the sun, too much to look at. All across the state, fields were going up in flames. One spark from a mower blade hitting a rock and the whole thing would go. Lucy reminded him several times a week that the tractor was strictly forbidden.

As he hefted each bale of hay across the field to a hayrack, the goats followed him, ripping off mouthfuls with their square little teeth. When they ran, their heavy udders tangled in their hind legs like big rubber balls. Sometimes they tripped, landing on top of them with a bounce, and Charlie would wince, afraid that one would pop like a balloon, spraying hot milk everywhere. The goats had yellow snake eyes and were the colors of stones: some brown, some gray, some white, some striped, sedimentary. They moved as one body. The kids, miniature versions of their mothers, scrambled to keep up and got punted around in the confusion. When he finally managed to get each bale forked into the big slatted hayracks, three or four goats leapt into each one and bedded down.

Lying in your food while you eat it, Charlie thought, stopping to catch his breath. Not such a bad idea. There were plenty of nights he was so exhausted that he wouldn't have minded doing it himself. The goats slit their yellow eyes blissfully, grabbing mouthfuls of whatever was in reach, while at the other end, their puckered assholes winked turds into it. Smart, Charlie thought, leaning on the pitchfork, but like most things the goats did, pretty damn stupid, too.

Out here in the field, the goats had become Charlie's constant companions, for better or for worse. He was responsible for their care and feeding, though Lucy did all the milking herself. "Men and milk don't mix," she told him on his first day. "Trust me, I've learned." She brought the does into the barn two by two early each morning, before Charlie was awake. Even the sound of the milk hitting the pail nauseated him. Why would anyone want to drink something that came out of the inside of a *goat*?

Once a week, Lucy loaded a big vat in the back of her truck and took the milk to town, where she sold it to the co-op. For a while, she had invited Charlie along with her, and he would scramble for an excuse not to go, but she had finally stopped asking. It wasn't a big town at all, not much bigger than Red Bank, but the longer he'd been on the farm, the more he felt panicky about it. He had spoken to hardly anyone except Lucy and the mailman for two months now. In his mind, town was a bewildering place, crowded, full of untranslatable signs and dangerous strangers. His own truck sat under some parched black walnut trees next to the barn, unused except for an occasional trip to the crossroads gas station, sticky from the dead dropped leaves. Lucy hated the truck, and she took every opportunity to remind him. Not that he could blame her. The truck would spit in your eye if it could. And it wasn't his, anyways. It was Darryl's.

You could say that Charlie had stolen it. But hadn't Darryl basically stolen it, too, from the old man down the road after they cut out half his lung, saying something about how he owed him? Jacked the tires, tinted the windows, and hung from the trailer hitch a pair of pink rubber testicles that swayed languorously when the truck was in motion and which Charlie hadn't had the nerve to touch, let alone remove.

The buck came up the hill slowly, bleating. He was a grizzled silver beast who could escape any fence, even though the fences were so tight, Lucy liked to say, that they could practically hold water. Lucy had long ago chained him to a tire to keep him in, and it bumped along behind him, kicking up a cloud of dust. He stopped to twist his body around and piss on his long white beard, then leveled his head at Charlie and looked him straight in the eye. "You old boogey!" Charlie shouted. The buck smelled like a bus station urinal. Often he would use his tire as a step stool, dragging it to the base of a pear tree and climbing up on it to get to the higher leaves. Then he would curl up in the center of it and go to sleep. Charlie had to give him some credit. He knew plenty of human beings who weren't smart enough to make the most of their lot in life.

His friends, for example. Back in Red Bank, his friends were complaining about how they couldn't find work, getting drunk every night and sponging off their girlfriends' waitressing tips. But not Charlie. Charlie had always known he would make it, as long as he stayed out of trouble. He picked up the trash in the yard, walked three miles to Shooters' to bring Darryl home when they called. He paid the bills. He cooked the meals. He broke the news and apologized to the neighbor when Darryl ran over her cat.

Charlie squeezed his water bottle over the back of his neck. He shook the memory away. A few more weeks. Then it was sayonara, goats. Sayonara, Lucy. A few more weeks and life would begin. When he got to the Gulf he'd drive that truck off a goddamn pier. And tell Darryl that he could just—no, tell Darryl nothing. That truck was never his. Charlie didn't have to answer for anything. He tightened his grip on the pitchfork and ground the tines into the dust.

Ah, shit. He lit a cigarette and took a long drag. Don't go there. It's over. It's behind you.

A brown and white doe looked up, opened her mouth, and let a hank of wet hay fall to the ground. *Eeh.*

The group that was clustered around the nearest hayrack looked up and joined in. *Eeh-eh-eh. Neh-eh-eh.* They crept towards him, stretching their necks towards the empty wheelbarrow.

"Boo!" Charlie yelled, knocking the wheelbarrow over, and they reared up and scattered. When he turned to right it, he felt a tug at his jeans. They had closed back in on him. One had already pulled the pack of cigarettes out of his back pocket and was gumming it to a pulp.

It was clearly a one-man job, feeding the crippled kid.

Charlie couldn't figure out why Lucy insisted he help her. Most of the time, she was shooing him off of things. "Never mind, Charlie," she would say, "just forget it," and snatch up the post hole digger and dig the post holes herself, or go back through the flower bed and weed it again as soon as he was done. He would vow to do better next time, and end up doing worse. She asked him to move the goats, and he put them in the pasture with the broken gate. They scattered and wasted their hay. He pulled flowers along with the weeds. The windows dried streaky.

But every day he and Lucy sat cross-legged in the shade of a pear tree in the paddock, knees almost touching, while the kid slurped its bottle between them, and Charlie had to admit that it was almost peaceful. The kid was pure white, with blue eyes in a little birdlike face and spindly crooked legs that could not support its body. When it was born, a few days after Charlie arrived, its mother got up and walked away, tripping over it. Now it bleated for her every time the herd came near the tree, trying to drag itself after them. The goats would turn their heads and regard it with disinterest, like people passing a bum on a sidewalk.

Lucy was convinced there still might be hope, if they could just get its strength up. She had shown Charlie how to hold it, how to stroke its neck to encourage it to swallow. When they were out there together feeding it, she talked about the farm, the state she and her ex-husband found it in when they moved down from the North twenty-five years before, and all the work they had done: the wall of briars they dug out of the pastures, the fences, the new roof they put on the farmhouse. She talked about her run-ins with the neighboring farmers— the Jesus boys, she called them—how they had waited all these years for her to give up and sell out, and how she had proven them all wrong.

"This pear tree," she said affectionately, waving a hand towards its branches. "When we got here this pear tree only came up to my thigh." She looked almost pretty, her narrow face tilted towards the kid, her long, dark hair in a braid down her back, her blue eyes and turquoise earrings electric against her tan skin. The wrinkles around her eyes softened them when she smiled. The silver rings on her fingers glinted in the sun. A few days after Charlie arrived, he realized that she used to be beautiful. It had just been a glimpse, a flash of understanding—mostly she seemed like she had been exactly the same forever. The farm seemed that way, too, as if it was frozen in time, under glass.

Lucy sighed and shook her head at herself, muttering something about her husband. Charlie, catching every few words, had the feeling that he was loping along behind a train, trying to grab hold and pull himself up and on.

"Decades. Entire decades gone to that asshole. And I begged him to stay. Why? I was scared. Meanwhile, he was dragging me to hell and back. Sometimes I wonder how I got out of it alive."

She took the empty bottle from Charlie, wiped the kid's chin with her thumb, and handed him another bottle. He tried to imagine the husband. At first he pictured someone like Darryl, slithering around in his greasy-backed chair in front of the TV with half a dozen empty beer cans at his feet. But of course he'd be nothing like Darryl. He'd be a Yankee with a college degree and glasses and a little beard. A different breed of asshole entirely.

Lucy leaned back and considered the kid, took the bottle from Charlie, and shook her head. "From your point of view, I imagine it all seems pretty damn foolish."

Charlie cleared his throat. It made a hollow sound. He moved his face into the shade, looked down at the kid's little face, the pink heart-shaped hooves that had never touched the ground, clean and soft as new pencil erasers. Look, Lucy, he wanted to say. You done what you did, and I don't know enough about it to judge one way or another. But she'd only shoot him one of those looks she was always giving him. He could tell her he knew exactly what it was like, living with someone like that, but he could imagine what she'd say to that: Oh, do you now? He ran his tongue over his dry lips and searched for something else.

"People is just—stupid." He winced as soon as he heard himself say it.

Lucy brushed a lock of hair off her forehead. "Now what the hell is *that* supposed to mean?"

Charlie shrugged and coughed into his fist, cast down his eyes to avoid her glare. He felt like scratching a hole in the dry dirt and climbing in. The kid nosed the bottle and burbled as if it was a baby—*their* baby. Charlie was starting to like the kid. It was the only thing on the place that had a sense of humor.

When Charlie arrived in June, Lucy was just recovering from kidding season and desperate for help. He was desperate, too—the truck had broken down just seventy-five miles out of Red Bank, like a final *fuck you* from Darryl, and he'd blown most of his money on a new starter when he found Lucy's help-wanted ad on a bulletin board at the gas station. He was grateful that she didn't ask questions. A week or two, tops, he thought, surveying the old frame farmhouse and rolling fields, deciding it might not be half bad. He had started to drag his duffel bag into the house, and Lucy shook her head and pointed up to the barn. He thought she was kidding. Then she gave him a foam mattress, a lamp, a few milk crates, and an armload of blankets and told him to make himself at home. "For real?" he said.

She gazed at him with those blue eyes, challenging him. "None of the others ever had a problem with sleeping in the barn."

You can do this, he told himself, lying on the floor of the grain room that first night, flies dropping from the rafters to land on his lips and the tinkling of the goats' bells waking him every time he started to nod off. Be a man, Charlie. Buck up. So she didn't seem to particularly like him. Who cares, he thought, so what? He was used to being misunderstood. He went about the world in two ways: there was the real Charlie, and then the Charlie he showed everyone else. He had learned never to say what he was thinking, because no one else was thinking the same thing. "Oh, yeah, Mr. Know-It-All?" Darryl would say when Charlie started speaking his mind. "I got news for you. You think you're so smart. Smarts ain't all you need, you know. Plenty of smart people end up cleaning up other people's shit for a living. So you just remember that, smart-ass."

There were women at home—mothers of his friends—who tried to take care of him. Let him spend school nights at their house, always tried to send him home with leftovers. He would sometimes warily accept their offers of kindness, but mostly he'd curl up tight as a pill bug until they left him alone. Refuse the hot dinner even when his stomach was rumbling with hunger. Shrug the friendly arm off his shoulders. He was determined to show everyone that he could take care of himself. If that meant being alone in the world—well, in the end we all are, aren't we?

"I'm afraid," Lucy said one blistering morning, "that we're going to have to put that kid out of its misery." Charlie had only just crawled out of the barn into the white sun. Lucy, done with the milking, was out front, watering a pitiful rosebush. Its flowerless branches were akimbo, as if reaching out for someone.

Charlie was clutching the barn radio. Lucy had bought it for him at the thrift shop in town, replaced the missing knobs with a pair of clamps, and declared it good as new, but it was always breaking, and he had brought it outside with the intention of working on it. He looked down at it as if he suddenly had no idea how it got into his hands. He could hear the kid out there, mewling under the pear tree. He could always hear it. It was just a matter of tuning it in or out. No, he thought. Hell no. He moved into a tiny patch of shade and scowled at her.

She shook a kink out of the hose, slapping the dry ground with it, ignoring his fixed gaze. "Fill a pail. That's the quickest way." Her voice was measured, matter-of-fact, like she was assigning him any old chore, weeding, spackling, that she knew he was bound to screw up. Don't talk to me like that, he thought, his grip tightening on the radio. I'm sick and tired of it.

"I've done this a dozen times. Trust me, Charlie. Above all it's got to be quick."

Quick, Charlie thought. Ha. When the male kids turned one month old, Lucy took each one and stretched a rubber band around its scrotum. "Go ahead," she said, as he watched in horror. "Call me the ball breaker. Just don't think you're the first genius to come up with it." Eventually, slowly, as the blood supply choked off, it all shriveled up and fell off like a scab. Charlie crept around the pasture for a week as if it was a minefield, terrified of seeing one or—worse—feeling one squash under his boot. Lucy caught him at it one day when he had squatted to examine what turned out to be a black walnut lying in the dust. "Don't be a baby!" she called across the fence, laughing at him. "Besides, you're never going to find one. The rats get them practically before they hit the ground."

The days were not quick—the fat sun heaving itself along above them. He thought of the buck, dragging his tire on the chain. Nothing on the place was quick—except the does, and only when they knew you wanted to catch them. Give the thing a chance, he thought. Give it a break. Just yesterday, hadn't it stood for a second? He started to fiddle with the radio, avoiding her eyes, his hands shaking. The antenna snapped off in his hand. He looked at it, dumbfounded.

"What are you doing with that?" Lucy snapped.

"What the hell does it look like? Trying to fix it."

"Fix it? Looks to me like you just broke it."

Charlie felt his ears and cheeks burn red. He looked up to meet her eye. "Well, goddamn! It's like everything else around here. If someone hadn't nigger-rigged it!"

Later, he regretted it. He regretted saying it and also what he did next, which was to turn and hurl the radio against the side of the barn. He regretted it because it was something Darryl would say and something Darryl would do. But mostly he regretted it because of the look on Lucy's face—that look of shock and superiority—the ammunition he'd given her for the case against him. She thought he was just another dumb redneck, didn't she? Well, he had news for her. She didn't know what the hell she was doing. She couldn't see past the end of her own nose. Always flipping through those stupid fashion magazines. Not even eating proper food. Making him sleep like an animal in the barn! And couldn't she see that there might be more than one way to do things? Was it really going to kill the goats if he fed them a half hour later than usual, or put the hay in three hayracks, instead of four? Maybe if she would ever just stop for a minute and try to see something from someone else's point of view, she would realize she didn't have it all figured out.

The next morning, when she left to pick up a load of hay, he followed her out to buy groceries at the gas station. If I only had the money, he thought, bumping down the long driveway, I would just keep going. I'd be gone so fast my sparks would set the field on fire. But then a panicky feeling came over him. The thought that it might take more than money. That it would take something that he did not have and could not earn, borrow, or steal.

He crossed the cattle guard with a jolt. From a distance, it looked like there was nothing keeping the goats in at this gap in the fence—and when you got close, you saw it was just a shallow ditch covered with loose metal bars spaced several inches apart. "How does it keep them in?" he asked Lucy when he arrived.

"If they try to cross it," she said, "they'll break their legs."

"And what if they break their legs?"

"They won't try."

"Why won't they try?"

"Because," she sighed impatiently, "because they're terrified of it."

Down at the gas station, he saw something that made him burn with jealousy: a boy and a girl in a truck with out-of-state plates, the back loaded up with furniture and boxes. The girl climbed out of the truck with a German Shepherd on a leash, looked around with disapproval, and walked the dog along the grass behind the phone booths. The boy leaned against the hood with a map for a while. Then she kissed him, and they climbed back in the truck. The dog jumped in after them, and they pulled out for who-knows-where. Charlie stood there, watching the bend in the road where they had disappeared, thinking, That should be my dog. That should be my girl. That should be me!

"You gonna buy something?" the old man behind the register finally barked. "Or you just gonna stand there and fog up my window like that?"

When he got back to the farm he went straight to the milking parlor and pulled a pail from a stack with a sound like a sword being pulled from a scabbard. There was a stamp on the bottom: BEST FOR MILKING—SEAMLESS AND STAINLESS. Charlie read it several times before turning it over and filling it with the hose. He moved quickly, afraid he'd lose his nerve. There are just certain obstacles, he told himself, that stand between me and the rest of my life. It is simply a matter of getting over and past them. He went out to the paddock, gathered up the kid in his arms, negotiating with its awkward legs. It was heavier than he thought it would be. Staggering towards the gate, he could feel its warm breath on his neck. It looked up at him. *Bah!*

Charlie stopped. What does she know, anyway, he thought, looking down at the little white body, the white eyelashes over the blue eyes, the soft hooves. The kid's knees were grass-stained from trying to drag itself along after the herd. *What the hell does she know better than me?* That's when he saw what he needed to do.

In the days before he left home, he had walked around feeling like a dam with a million gallons of water pressed up behind him. Acting like nothing was different, taking Darryl on his midnight beer run, making plans with his friends, all the while the money he'd withdrawn from the bank sealed in an envelope in his dresser drawer, a secret he held under his tongue like a pebble.

The secret now was the kid, hidden away under a locust tree at the foot of a hill in the back corner of the farthest pasture, where Lucy never went. Alive. Charlie was going to heal it. Prove Lucy wrong once and for all. She had been so grateful when he lied and told her that he'd done it—she had even reached out to hug him—that for a moment he felt a loop of doubt in his gut. But *just wait until it's up and walking*, Charlie thought that night, lying on his mattress on the floor, listening to the jangling of the bells. *Wait until I lead it up to the paddock, healthy and strong on four legs.* She would have to reconsider everything she thought she knew about him.

Every day, he went down to feed it, sitting in the shade where the kid had scratched out a shallow hole in the dust. One morning, propping it up with one finger under its belly, he managed to get it to stand. "There!" he said. The kid looked around, pleased with itself. But as soon as he pulled his hand away, it crumpled. He tried again. The sun ratcheted up the sky, pulling away the shade of the tree. "Just another little while yet," Charlie told the kid, and the kid shook its ears in agreement.

Weeks dragged on. The heat would not let up. Rain did not come. Every day, without fail, the sky was cruel blue and cloudless. Birds panted in the trees. The goats stood around on their skinny legs, heaving like accordions.

"Fuck the sun." Lucy stood on the porch of the house in her bathrobe with a cup of steaming coffee. The outside cats were scratching at the door to be let in to the shade of the house, while the inside cats were scratching to escape the oven of the living room. Charlie was working behind her, up on a chair, washing the windows with vinegar. She said it slowly. "Fuck. The. Sun." Then stood there, tapping her foot. He got the feeling that she was waiting for him to apologize for it.

She went on, "The weather never used to be like this. It's freakish. You know, I think it's got to be more than just the greenhouse effect. I think we might possibly be getting *closer* to the sun. And I'll tell you what's scary. If it's this hot now, what's it going to be like in fifty years?" She sighed. Charlie felt a darkness close in around the edges of his vision. Fifty years—where on earth would he be in *fifty* years?

"Well, it's you kids I feel sorry for. A future like that. My God, all *we* had to worry about was blowing ourselves up. Now you—*you've* got problems." She crossed her arms, balanced her coffee cup in the crook of her elbow, and contemplated the yard. Charlie crumpled the newspaper he'd been using as a rag, sat down on the chair, and lit a cigarette, trying to shake off the darkness around his eyes. Why is everyone always dooming me? The cats leapt up into the busted-out rockers and shit-riddled flower boxes. He watched, resisting the urge to toss a boot at them. Spoiled, he thought. Damn cats.

Lucy turned around and eyed his cigarette. "Those things will kill you, you know. You should quit."

"What for?" he muttered. "Gonna die anyway."

Lucy snorted. Charlie smiled a little, pleased to at least make her laugh, for once, even if he hadn't intended to. She turned back towards the yard and motioned with her coffee cup towards the truck sitting under the walnut trees. Her voice turned gentle, coaxing. "That truck's not yours, is it, Charlie?"

Charlie swallowed, feeling the fumes of the vinegar in his throat. He thought of the milking pail—seamless and stainless. That's what I am, he thought. Fresh start. Brand new.

"Sure it is."

Lucy turned and rolled her eyes. "Come on, Charlie. Rubber testicles? You somehow don't seem quite the type."

Charlie had the sensation of a door swinging on loose hinges—whether opening or closing, he could not tell. The feeling of pivoting between gas pedal and brake, trying to make a split-second decision about stopping for a hitchhiker at sixty miles per hour. He could tell her the whole story. Go back to the day when he was five and Darryl first hit him across the mouth with a beer bottle. But what would be the use?

"Why?" He edged his voice into a challenge. "You got a problem with my truck?"

Lucy looked at him a second longer, shrugged, raised her eyebrows, and brushed past him into the house, shaking her finger at a spot he'd missed as she passed the window.

I don't know about no greenhouse effect, he thought, leaning forward, elbows on knees, to spit between his boots. All I know is that it's too damn hot. Too hot to think or even take a breath. A flock of geese passed over the field. For the past few days it had seemed as if every time he looked up, there were geese up there. As if it was the same flock, circling the globe, searching for a cool place to touch down. Not finding one.

The milk went bad. It was something that the goats were eating. "It was absolutely fine," Lucy told him, pouring a white torrent into the barn sink, "except that it tasted like shit." With no milk, the little money that had been coming in dried up completely. Every morning, Lucy still had to bring in the heavy-uddered does, and every morning Charlie lay on his mattress and listened to the sound of her pouring the milk down the drain. He watched her stalk the fence line in a floppy straw hat and sandals, searching for the culprit weed. He searched the pasture himself, not knowing what he was looking for, but wanting to save the day.

He always managed to salvage enough milk from the bottom of the pails to fill a bottle for the kid. Every evening, when he reached the crest of the hill, he crossed his fingers for the sight of it standing. But it was always in the exact same spot he had left it—though each day a little bigger, plump and full like a summer cloud. A dream, a frosted shining birthday cake in the burnt field. Charlie would kneel and massage its tiny legs, shaking doubt off the way the goats shook off flies.

Lucy drove farther and farther to find anyone who would sell her hay, coming back with an empty gas tank, a sweat-drenched shirt, and four bales she paid sixty dollars for. The goats would finish it in minutes, the buck dragging his tire up and muscling through the crowd, lowering his head and sliding his horns under the kids like a forklift, tossing them out of the way. Afterwards they would all jostle up to the barn to chew the fence slats. Their ribs were starting to show.

Lucy and Charlie stopped speaking to one another. They communicated in grunts, only when necessary, and went through whole days without crossing paths. They drew down into survival mode, just like the trees. Days turned into weeks, and Charlie lost all sight of any world that might exist beyond the farm. Then one night in September, while he cooked himself a can of beans and Lucy, who seemed to have quit eating altogether, sat at the kitchen table riffling through one of her glossy magazines, she broke the silence.

"Trash," she said, throwing the magazine down and pushing her chair back. "Why do I read this trash?"

Charlie froze. Was he supposed to answer that? He steeled himself for whatever was coming next—he was making a racket with the spoon, or his beans were stinking up the house, or he was breathing too loud.

"I'll tell you something. Those Jesus boys. They hate a goat. I *know* they've got plenty of hay back there in their barns. But now that the stuff's as good as gold, they just don't want to see it go to a goat. Cows? Yes. Horses, sure. But wait till old Lucy drives up wanting a few bales for her goats—then it's 'No deal, ma'am, sorry I can't help you, but I sure can't. Why don't you try on down the road?'"

"Don't call them that," Charlie said. He'd been so ready for an insult that this one seemed directed at him. And it was, wasn't it? She looked down her nose at *everybody*.

"Why not?" She turned to him, seeming genuinely to want to know.

Charlie shrugged, thrown off guard. "It ain't right," he said lamely.

She turned away, slapped her hand on the magazine, pulled it back towards herself, and opened it. "Well, Charlie? I wonder what they call *me*? Twenty-five years they've kept me shut out. Not a single one of them has ever offered me a hand. Sniffing around this place like vultures, wondering when I'm going to throw in the towel. Meanwhile, half the time I'm out here with no help, and there's just simply some things a woman can't do by herself."

Really? he thought. That's not what *you* say. He shifted his weight. "Still ain't right."

She let out a violent rush of air, put her hands on top of her head. "This is not an easy life, Charlie. It is one hell of a life. I'll tell you, when I was your age"— she looked at him—"how old are you?"

"Eighteen." Here it comes, he thought, putting his spoon down and clenching his fist. All right. Give me the lecture. Tell me I should go home. Go on. I can take whatever you've got.

She looked up towards the ceiling, as if searching for something. "Eighteen. When I was your age—no, maybe a little older—I thought I had figured out the secret. My parents' life, it was a trap, I could see that. All about appearances. They were just consumed with keeping up appearances. My father worked himself to death so we could live in the right neighborhood. And my mother. God, my mother. Cocktail parties and bridge games. She had these guest towels—the guest linens, she called them—and she took them out of the closet and ironed them and put them out in every bathroom when company was coming over. It seemed like that was all she was ever doing—unfolding the ironing board to iron the guest linens, hanging them up, folding them up, and putting them back in the closet—and God forbid anyone should ever use these towels to actually dry their *hands*.

"The thing was, all my friends were buying into it. Getting married straight out of college, moving into houses just like their mothers' with a monogrammed set of towels all their own. Not me. Oh, no. I was too smart for that. I got out. I started new. Never mind that I wouldn't have any money. I'm going to live simply, I told myself. I'm going to live simply and close to the land. Get my hands dirty and find real satisfaction, and I found a man who said that was what he wanted, too.

"But it turns out—it turns out. One more year, I always tell myself, one more year and it will be running like clockwork. Every year I think, just make it through kidding season, Lucy. And then kidding season comes, and something happens like that little white kid, and it takes years off my life. *Years.* No matter how hard you work, it's a gamble and the house always wins. Like the weather. Lord. I don't think we'll ever see rain again."

Charlie felt flushed and disoriented, not sure which way was up, the feeling of falling in a dream. What was she trying to say to him? "It will break sometime," he mumbled, failing in his attempt to sound like a man. Wasn't that what she wanted him to do? Comfort her?

She let the magazine slap shut. "Of course it will, Charlie. Don't think I don't know that. I've been at this longer than you've been alive. Of course it will break. That's not the point. It will break and then it will dry up and then it will break again. They'll stop eating whatever it is they're eating out there and the milk will get back to normal and there'll be money coming in again. So it goes. That's not the point. The point is, Charlie, we're in for a hell of a fall."

We? Charlie looked around the kitchen in a panic. *We?*

A week later Lucy headed out to Georgia on a tip she'd gotten on some cheap hay. She would be gone overnight, staying with friends, and her preparations for leaving had the feeling of a much larger event. Early that morning, she checked and triple-checked things up at the barn, made long lists for Charlie on the backs of envelopes. She put makeup on.

Charlie followed her around, nodding as she ticked off instructions, biting his tongue and reminding himself that for twenty-four blessed hours, he would have the place to himself. Lucy was like he'd never seen her, giddy with excitement.

Finally, satisfied with everything, she went up to her truck and threw her bag in the back. Charlie stood a few feet away, shaded his eyes, and lit a cigarette, watching.

One foot on the running board, she turned. "Let me have two of those."

He raised his eyebrows and shook two cigarettes out of the pack, stepping forward. She plucked them out of his hand and then pointed them at him. She narrowed her eyes, but her voice was playful. "I don't want to hear one word out of you. Not one word. I'm entitled to two cigarettes every once in a while." She held them up in front of her nose. "One to get me to Georgia. And one to get me back." She tucked one behind each ear and smiled at him.

Charlie smiled back. He held up his hands. "I ain't saying nothing."

She got in the truck and pulled the door shut. "Listen," she said, rolling down the window and smiling again. "Try not to burn the place down, all right?"

Charlie raised his hand again to shade his eyes, squinting into the morning sun. He felt fifty pounds lighter, celebratory. He grinned. "Can't be making no guarantees."

.   .   .

As the hours wore on, his freedom turned into a burden, and Charlie was overwhelmed by the mounting pressure to make the most of his time. After morning chores, he ended up sleeping most of the day, sweating, the blanket over his face to keep off the flies. In the afternoon he went down to the house to watch television, but the only thing he could find was the local news. A church full of men, clasping hands and swaying, prayed for rain. A ticker at the bottom of the screen reported over and over that there had been three heat-related deaths in a town just twenty miles away. Charlie stared blankly at the screen. He could not draw the connection between the world of those men in the church and the world of the farm, between the heat that beat on the barn and the fields and the heat that was killing people—*killing* people—right down the road.

He switched the TV off. Why bother praying, anyway? What good was that going to do? What you had to do was take things in your own hands. Write your own story. God or anybody wasn't going to just *give* it to you.

He got up and walked around. Creaking under his feet, the floorboards were hot, as if embers were smoldering beneath them. He had a strange sensation that the place itself was judging him. Even the furniture seemed to watch him with critical eyes.

He made a sudden turn and, feeling bold, walked down the hall to Lucy's bedroom. He had never been inside, but he had seen, from the yard, the air-conditioning unit in her window, and had envied the sound night's sleep he imagined she got in the cool air.

When he opened the door, an orange-and-white flash of fur sprung out at him, and he wheeled around as if he had sprung a booby trap, expecting to see her in the hall behind him. Go on, he told himself, his heart pounding. She's miles and miles away.

The bed—unmade, a nest of green and yellow daisy print sheets, an old tattered quilt, one pillow—was just a mattress on the floor, not much thicker than his own foam pad in the barn. He sat down on it. A sheet of plywood half covered a broken floorboard. Another cat slit its eyes at him from a pile of clothes in the corner. The air conditioner was unplugged, sagging, covered with dust, and obviously hadn't worked in years. The afternoon sun streamed in through the window. It was hot in there.

Though it shocked him to realize, it was somehow sexy, too, in the way that the few girls' rooms he'd been in were all sexy—the bra tossed carelessly on the chair, the mysterious jars and bottles on the nightstand. Mostly, though, it made him sad—the vase of withered wildflowers that should have been thrown out weeks ago, fruit flies hovering over it, the stack of well-leafed magazines on the floor—and the sadness and sexiness all wrapped up together confused him. An old pack of cigarettes was hidden in an enameled box next to the bed. Hidden from who? He picked up a corner of the quilt and let it drop. He smelled unwashed sheets, a faint scent of Lucy's shampoo, her sweat, the goat stench that he had long since stopped noticing on himself. Her smell had become so familiar to him that it gave him a wave of nostalgia, as if he was remembering it from somewhere long ago. He felt so lonely that, for a minute, he wished she was there.

Ah, come on, he thought, and stood up. Come on, Lucy. He kicked at the pile of laundry. You didn't have to settle for this. What are you trying to prove? He pulled a dresser drawer open with a jerk and rooted around behind the clothes. Opened another, and then another, then turned back to the pile of clothes strewn on the floor. In the pocket of a pair of jeans, he found a wad of bills. He smoothed them out with shaking hands and counted them. Less than the price of a tank of gas. Would hardly get him over the state line. He stuffed them into his pocket anyway. "Sorry, Lucy," he said aloud, realizing as he said it that he mostly meant it. But you owe me, he thought, kicking the clothes back into a pile and thinking of Darryl. Best advice that asshole ever gave me. It ain't stealing when you're owed.

Back up at the barn, his heart pounding, feeling rotten and hollow as an old stump, he walked in on a scene of destruction. The goats had broken into his room.

They did it to spite me, he thought, frozen in the doorway. Not out of hunger. Out of pure spite. The grain bags in the corner were ripped and torn, feed scattered everywhere. There was a hole chewed in his duffel bag, bullet-shaped turds in his clothes. They had pissed all over the mattress, left the sheets in a tangle. As if they had gathered there for a final victory dance.

They'd been planning it. He reached down for his chewed-up sunglasses and then let them drop again to the floor. They'd just been biding their time.

He walked out of the barn. The sun was setting red over the hills. The house glared at him. There was not a single welcoming corner of the place, nowhere to take shelter. He went back into the barn, pulled the sheets off the mattress, dragged it into the yard, and soaked it with the hose. He threw the sheets on the burn pile, though there had been a burn ban on for months. He went into the paddock and nailed a two-by-four across the splintered board where they'd broken through the wall. The goats were in a nervous cluster under the pear tree, eyeing him. He swept his arm into the air and shouted and they took off down the hill.

The mattress dried fast in the last light of the day, but when dark finally fell and he lay down to sleep on it, it still reeked of piss. He tried to sleep anyway, desperate to escape for a few hours. He squeezed his eyes shut. With no sheets to pull up over his face, the flies dropped to his lips. Mice scurried over his legs, then something bigger. The goats had made their way back up to the paddock. He could hear them out there, rubbing their bodies against the dry wall of the barn. He heard their bells, the drag of the buck's tire and chain. The buck began to scrape his horns back and forth along the wall, a tin cup along the bars of a cell. Back and forth, back and forth, until the sound seemed like it was coming from inside Charlie's skull. He covered his ears but still heard it. *Come out!* they were saying. Charlie lay still, afraid to move or make a sound. *Come out!* He reached down and groped for the sheets, forgetting there were no sheets. *Come out! Come out! Or we are coming in!*

An hour or so before dawn he got up and ran. As if pulled by a greater force. Crossing the yard towards the truck in the dark he was cool as a breeze in the night air.

Charlie made it to the Gulf a couple of months after hurricane season. When he first saw the blue-gray water, he went down to the beach and dipped his hand in, to be sure he wasn't dreaming. He found a job his first week, working construction on new condominiums along the shore. He made good money, enough to rent a place of his own. After a few months, he was promoted to assistant foreman, if only because he was the one native speaker of English on the crew. From the men he worked with, he picked up a little Spanish—mostly words having to do with the weather, because it was what everyone talked about on the job.

The winter was mild, even for the Gulf, warm and still. After work they would all go down to a bar at the old marina that didn't bother to check IDs. Charlie usually bought the first round. They would sit out on the deck for hours and Charlie would look out at the piers and the few boats in the water and marvel at his good fortune. Sometimes he still couldn't believe he'd made it. He heard that the southeast had been hit with freak snowstorms, record lows, ice that snapped power lines. Who's too close to the sun now? he thought, but fought a feeling of unease at the wild swings of extremes. When he heard a special report on the radio one night at the bar about a blizzard there, he couldn't even picture the place they were talking about. Still, he whistled through his teeth, as if he'd made a close call. *Está nevando,* he said to the others at the table, and pointed north, because he hadn't learned the word for *home.*

One day at the bar in April, in the first hint of the tropical heat to come, Charlie, half drunk, pulled off his shirt and announced he was going in the water. As the others whooped and cheered, he took off his boots, stepped off the deck, and jogged out onto the echoing pier. Above the water, white gulls circled. He looked up at them, then down at his pale feet slapping the warm planks of the pier, then down through the cracks to the dark water below. He stopped short, yanked back by a thought that grabbed like the barbs of a fish hook in the back of his neck.

How many days? How many days did the kid fix its eyes on the crest of the hill, waiting for him? And Lucy, out checking the fence line for winter damage, how many steps did she take towards what was left of it, first thinking it was nothing but a last dirty pile of snow?

The men back at the table watched him. They wondered why he stood there, staring down through the planks, rather than diving in. *Se le perdió algo,* they said to one another after a while. *He has lost something.*

Shadow on a Weary Land

It was Frank James, not Jesse, who buried the treasure in Brown's Ridge. This is what the Musician tells me as he pulls the metal detector out the back of his pickup and slings it over his shoulder. We find a deer path through the woods behind his cabin and take the back way up the ridge. The Musician breaks through low branches and lopes up the steep, loose ground. *But Frank didn't have half as much dough,* I say, out of breath when we get to the top. To the south, the Nashville skyline crouches on the horizon like a stalking animal. *But he was smarter,* the Musician grins. *He planned ahead. For future generations,* I say. *Exactly,* the Musician says, tapping the end of his nose.

Life in Brown's Ridge is like this: At night, the howl of the coyotes can split you in two. In the morning, the sun is slow to rise over the spine of the ridge, and starlings and wild turkeys pick their way across the dark fields and into the trees. When the coyotes come by, Greenup Bird lifts his old head and howls, overcome by something ancient inside him. The woods hold pockets of cool air in the summer and warm air in the winter, and walking through them you tend to look over your shoulder, thinking something is following you. On the steepest parts of the ridge there are oaks and hickories over three hundred years old, saved from generations of loggers by their inaccessibility. Up there I have seen bald eagles, bucks with antlers like coatracks. In the valley below, Katy Creek rushes south to the Cumberland. Brown's Ridge Pike runs beside it, all the way to Kentucky. Out there on the horizon, Nashville seems to be hundreds of miles away. Not many people live here: less people than cows, less people than copperheads, coyotes, possums. They call it Brown's Ridge after Kaspar Brown, the first man killed by Indians here. No one knows when exactly, but that was sometime around 1799.

The Musician and I have lived here since 1985, and never before has there been any talk of treasure. I can't believe that no one has thought to look for it yet, in the same way I can't believe that the Nashville developers have only now discovered Brown's Ridge. When Joe Guy's father bought his farm in 1935, the James brothers had only been gone sixty years. There were people around who remembered passing them on the road, seeing them at the horse races, smiling to their wives. It's a wonder that it never occurred to Joe Guy to look for some sort of a treasure buried somewhere on his thousand-acre tract. Or to anyone else, for that matter: the families in the trailers on the other side of the ridge, the dairy farmers, the kids in grubby T-shirts who miss the school bus day after day. Lacy, the pretty young waitress at the Meat 'n' Three, talks every once in a while about striking it rich in the new state lottery, buying a plane ticket to New York. Even Preacher Jubal Cain would not be above scratching around in the dirt for a few thousand dollars' worth of gold. So why are we the first? The Musician says *None of them would have even known where to look.* The woods are quiet, the hot hush of late summer as it turns into fall. *Have you got a map?* I ask him. *Don't need one,* he says, handing me a shovel. *I got Dave.*

Since he showed up on the Musician's doorstep last winter, Dave has claimed to have a direct line to the spirit of Jesse James. He is quick to point out that it is not Jesse's ghost, that he is in heaven and is not among us. The first time Jesse spoke to him, Dave was lying on the Musician's floor, and he sat up and said, *Holy shit, the Lord speaketh,* and Jesse said, *No, man, listen, it's Jesse James.* Last week, over an after-dinner joint, Dave told the Musician that Jesse said that his brother's treasure was buried somewhere along the ridgeline. *Can Jesse be any more specific?* the Musician asked, taking a hit. *No, man,* Dave said, exhaling a cloud of smoke. *I don't want to bug him.* Dave believes the end of the world is coming any time now. *As in the book of Revelation?* I ask him. *Fuck Revelation,* he says. *I'm talking Old Testament here. Isaiah, man. He saw it all.* He keeps the book of Isaiah tucked in his coat pocket, torn from a Bible he stole out of a church. The pages are held together with duct tape. When I first met Dave, I thought he was a homeless guy the Musician had taken in, like a stray cat, but then he pulled a fancy cell phone from a holster on his belt and took a call from his girl in California. *She's got the vision,* he says, pointing between his eyes. *She's got it better than me.* Every Sunday, at Brown's Ridge Baptist church, Jubal Cain preaches Jesus' love. Outside the church is a sign that says: HOT OUTSIDE? WE'VE GOT PRAYER CONDITIONING! And beneath that it says, YOU ARE WELCOME. COME AS YOU ARE. When Preacher Jubal slows his Oldsmobile at the stop sign by my house and I happen to be outside, he looks long and hard but does not wave. I've never set foot inside Brown's Ridge Baptist, and neither has Dave. Dave's cell phone ring plays "Dixie." He uses the pages of Revelation to roll his joints.

None of us can claim to belong here. The Musician and I came to Nashville in the seventies, him for the drugs and the music, me just for the drugs. We got to be friends, or at least were always showing up at the same parties. He was young and knew the good-looking girls. I was forty years old, just getting started on the heavy stuff. When the scene vibed out in the eighties, we both decided to move to Brown's Ridge. Way out to the country, we thought back then. Dave's from California or Nevada or somewhere, no one really knows. I always thought Lacy was born here, but it turns out she moved up with her momma from South Carolina when she was a few years old. Preacher Jubal Cain is from Bowling Green, Kentucky. Joe Guy's daddy, when he bought the farm, moved down from Paradise Ridge, a good twenty miles to the north. Frank and Jesse James came from Missouri via Muscle Shoals, Alabama. Brown, before he was pierced through the heart with an arrow, was a Yankee from Philadelphia, forging his way south to find a better life for his family. The only person I know who is actually from Brown's Ridge is Joe Guy Jr., born the year we moved here, in the upstairs bedroom of his daddy's big white house, but he cut out of here two years ago, and no one's heard from him since.

The metal detector that the Musician bought is cheap and unreliable. There is no depth setting and for the first few days he wastes hours digging up beer cans and pop tabs that lie just beneath the leaf litter. Every morning he knocks on my door and me and Greenup Bird go with him up the ridge. Dave comes, too, and we all help dig. The Musician points to a spot and I go at it with a short-handled spade while Greenup goes at it with his claws and teeth, dirt spraying out behind him through his back legs. Since the stroke, my left arm shakes so badly that it's difficult to control any tool. I get tired easily and have to sit down. Greenup is named for the victim of the first peacetime bank robbery in this country, which went down in Liberty, Missouri, in 1866. I live by the creek in a house that J. D. Howard, a local grain dealer known to be a gambler, built in 1875. The house has fifteen-foot-high ceilings and a fireplace in every room. Across the Pike is the field where J. D. Howard kept his horse, an exceptionally fine animal for a man of his humble profession. On weekdays developers trawl through Brown's Ridge in their Hummers, wider than one lane of the road. They pull over to ask directions, looking down at us through mirrored sunglasses, and we point them the wrong way. I found Greenup Bird on the Pike two years ago, half-starved and half-dead, a cross between a God-knows-what and a Lord-have-mercy. He's got one blue eye and one black and a coat that feels like a wire brush. As the Musician says, he is one plug-ugly dog. We make a good pair, him and me.

The Musician once played bass for a famous band. He's been all over the world and he's got luggage stuffed in every closet in the cabin. He's got stories, whether you choose to believe them or not. He's played to a crowd of twenty thousand in Berlin, slept with a one-armed Haitian girl in the back of a Spanish club. The Musician's given name is Randy Spaulding, but when he started touring he had it legally changed to Lex Spark. He's got good days and bad days, and when I go to see him I usually know which one it is before I'm halfway up his mud-rutted drive. On bad days he stays inside the dark musty cabin, tending to his regret like it's a pot on the stove. On good days he is electric with plans, plans you wouldn't think he had in him, like searching for Frank James's treasure. He built the cabin himself, with lumber he talked various people into giving him. Three years ago, it was the Musician who broke into my house, dragged me out of a puddle of piss and shit, and drove me to the hospital, where after three days in a coma they told me I was a very lucky man. He hasn't been able to get session work in Nashville in years. An upright bass leans against his kitchen counter like a woman trying to catch a bartender's eye. He won't touch it. I imagine he doesn't play music anymore for the same reason I don't do drugs anymore: you can only push up to the edge so many times before you realize the one thing on the other side is your own mortality, with no one waiting there to keep your grave clean.

It's impossible to prove, but most people would agree that it was Jesse James, alias J. D. Howard, who shot Greenup Bird at that bank in Missouri, committing one of the first crimes of a lifetime of infamy. It was ten years before he moved to Brown's Ridge and changed his name, built his high-ceilinged house, and tried to live the life of an honest man. Frank James, when he arrived soon after with his wife and young son, took the name of B. J. Woodson and rented a farm along the creek. Joe Guy's thousand-acre farm, the biggest tract in the entire county, was sold quietly this summer, in the middle of June. When the work crews started rolling in, Preacher Jubal Cain watched the surveyor's tape go up and said, *Whosever will, let him come. A time of prosperity is here.* We dig deep holes along the ridgeline, some because of a sign from the metal detector, some because Dave rolls his eyes back in his head and points, some for no reason at all. As we dig we call out to each other through the trees: *You got anything? Nothing, man. You? Nothing.*

My mind, before I ruined it, was a beautiful thing. As an old man I can say this without vanity or pride. The brilliance was like the light of late day over Joe Guy's back field, but now the light is gone. What's left are the scraps, held together with wire and string. Nothing has grown back in the ruts of the drugs. I used to be an inventor. I've sold dozens of patents for things you use every day. I like to think I have made life easier for people, better. Some nights I think I can feel Jesse's bootsteps if I lean off my mattress and press my fingers to the floor, but it is only the rumble of the trucks coming down the Pike. Living in a place like this, you would think it would be easy to start believing in ghosts. But I am haunted by something more real than ghosts. Behind the Minute Mart, on a scrubby lot where the gas trucks turn around, two perfect rows of daffodils come up year after year, just wide enough to line the drive of a farmhouse of which there is no longer a trace. Whoever planted those daffodils, a woman, I picture, in a homemade dress, did it decades ago, without any thought of me. The Musician drives me into town to cash my Social Security checks and buy new boots, and I hold my left arm down with my right to keep it from jerking out and hitting the gear shift. Every once in a while, I'll speak a whole sentence backwards, and the woman at the bank will smile at me with false patience, like I'm a little boy. We used to go to the honky-tonks on Saturday nights to tell stories about the old days and complain about the music, but we don't go out at night anymore, because the headlights on the Musician's truck quit. He's working part-time laying tile. Days are rough for a self-employed tradesman, what with all the cheap labor the contractors can scare up. The Musician looks down at his boots, the steel toes showing through big holes in the worn-out leather. He sighs and says, *It's a tough row to hoe.*

Dave won't touch the metal detector. He thinks it is a blasphemy. He says that God will disconnect his line to Jesse if he gets too greedy. *If you ask, you shall receive,* he tells us, and many days when we go out digging he stays behind at the cabin, leaning back on the porch steps with a joint. *Jesse might want to get in touch with me,* he says. *You two go on ahead.* When we come back in the afternoon he is curled up snoring in a patch of sun. We've happened on a cobalt blue medicine bottle, which the Musician is certain we can sell at an antique shop in town. We've found a lug nut, an old snarl of baling wire, eighteen broken Coke bottles, a hornet's nest, a hollow tree that the Musician climbed inside of and looked all the way up to the sky. We found an old shoe, a ladder, a cracker tin, but still no treasure. *Jesse's not sure yet if he really wants you to find it,* Dave says when we wake him. *Well, tell Jesse to make up his mind,* the Musician says. *We haven't got much time.* At dusk I walk Greenup Bird through the hay fields of Joe Guy's farm, letting him scare up rabbits and bark at the deer. I find a dead raccoon hanging from its neck in the crook of a beech tree. I wonder how many more times we'll walk through the field: five more mornings, ten. I tell the raccoon, *You're lucky to get out now.* I rub out surveying marks spray-painted on the grass with my heel.

One morning in mid-September we think we've hit the jackpot. After a clear sign from Jesse, Dave starts in on a level stretch of the hillside, alongside the grade of an old logging road. A foot and a half down his shovel strikes metal, and we all rush over to him, Greenup panting, slapping our legs with his tail. With his hands in the air the Musician circumscribes the size of Confederate bills, bars of solid gold. The shovel twangs encouragingly. But what we dig up turns out to be a sheet of rusted tin hinged to a spiraled copper pipe from an old still. The Musician slumps his shoulders for a moment, then gets back to work. He's tall and lanky and loose the way a bass player should be. He eats and eats but stays skinny as a whip. He feeds me and Dave in the cabin most nights, frying hamburgers when he's got work, boiling potatoes when he doesn't. Dave chucks the pipe downhill. In the twenties, the ridge had more bootleggers than any other place in the county: so wild and steep, yet so close to town. They kept little fox dens at the foot of trees where they sometimes spent the night. They pinned pictures of Clara Bow to the sycamores and ate the lunches their wives packed them in tin pails, throwing the chicken bones over their shoulders. The ones without women sometimes moved out here for good, squatting on unclaimed land in tar paper shacks. In the deepest hollers we find the last of these places, abandoned by the gangs of teenage boys who once used them as clubhouses. Behind their graffiti and karate posters, the walls are insulated with layers of newspaper from the 1950s. We peel them off and read the ads for land auctions and farm liquidations, and I think about how this cashing in on the country is not any kind of new thing.

In 1969 Brown's Ridge damn near went. Joe Guy's father saw the development going on in the rest of the county and made up his mind to sell. He found someone in Clarksville who would buy his herd of Holsteins, mapped out roads, and even had sewer lines put into the front field. The caps are still out there; sometimes I trip over them when Greenup and I walk at sunset, or Joe Guy's mower catches a blade and from my bedroom I hear the scrape of metal against metal. In the spring of that year, Joe Guy's father stood at the edge of the field with a notary public, a man from a development company, and blueprints for two- and three-bedroom brick ranch houses spread out on the hood of his Cadillac. He was all set to sign the final papers when he had a heart attack and dropped right where he stood, into the ditch on the side of the road. The pen fell out of his hand. The man from the development company said it was as if he had been struck by lightning. *Almost like an act of God,* he would tell people for the rest of his life. The farm and all the land, as drawn up in the will, went to the sole heir, Joe Guy, and Joe refused to sell. He bought the cows back from the man in Clarksville

and put them right back out in the pasture, kept on farm-
ing for the next thirty years. But now Joe is older than his
father was when he dropped into the weeds that day, and he's
got visions of Florida dancing in his eyes, clean fingernails,
sleeping late.

Some days, if either of us has some money, the Musician
and I get lunch down at the Meat 'n' Three. Lacy pours our
coffee and sings along to the country video station on the
TV. She holds her check pad up to her mouth and whispers
not to order the fish. *The cat done licked it,* she says. The
Musician eats fried chicken with okra, cottage cheese, pinto
beans. I eat cornbread and a biscuit and take my rainbow of
pills. Lacy is young enough to be the Musician's daughter,
my granddaughter. She wears a wide black belt low on her
hips, jeans, bright blue eye shadow. She's got the body of a
1950s movie star. The Musician watches her carefully as she
moves around the room. Most days, she'll sit down with us
while we eat, stealing a French fry or a potato chip from the
Musician's plate, snapping her fluorescent gum. But these
days the place is packed with developers up from Nashville,
spreading out topo maps on the tables and picking the pork
out of their turnip greens. Joe Guy comes in with a pretty
lady in panty hose and a suit. They sit at the counter and go
over a brochure of computer-generated images of big brick
houses. *We're going to call it Apple Orchard Acres,* she tells
him, and he rubs his hands together and nods. Lacy brings

his sweet tea and asks if he's heard from Joe Jr. He only smiles and winks at her. His brand-new F-350 is parked outside the restaurant, the engine ticking. *Wouldn't you do it, too?* the Musician asks, when he sees me looking. *Wouldn't you do the same, for a couple million dollars?* What would I do with two million dollars? Buy back the land. Save it for the coyote, the heron, the possum, the bobcat, the kestrel, the broad-winged hawk.

Since my stroke, this is what I have come to know: The path to enlightenment is free of all desire. The doctors say it is something to do with a drop in my testosterone levels, but I feel it is something greater. I look at the world with a new, pure love. The graders rumble down the Pike and pull into Joe Guy's front fields, laying down the roads. There are three phases of development planned, 188 houses total, with talk of a golf course. The smaller farmers in town, when they hear about it, start to reassess their mortgages, talk to their wives. Dave doesn't want me and the Musician to get left behind at the Second Coming. He prays for us to find Jesus. But I don't need to. *I've found love without him,* I say. I look for other answers, other explanations. I read whatever I can get my hands on. Every mammal on earth, I've read, from mouse to man to mammoth, goes through roughly the same number of heartbeats in a lifetime. When I tell this to Dave, he says, *If that's not proof of God, then I sure as hell don't know what is.*

We dig up a mule shoe, six square-headed nails, a milking pail, a barrette. We find an old Maytag washer, rusted parts all tumbled down the hillside like spilled guts. I have a certain respect for folks who chucked their garbage out their back door. When I was lying unconscious in the hospital, the Musician came into my house and cleaned out as much junk as he could, the boxes of old syringes, the rank buckets of piss. When I relearned how to talk, the first thing I said was, *Thank you.* Jesse James and a member of his posse, a man named Bill Ryan, alias Tom Hill, drank beer and ate tinned oysters at the saloon that once stood on the site of the Minute Mart, which keeps its security lights on all day and all night, too. We stop to buy Cokes and cellophane-wrapped miniature chess pies, which keep us going until midnight. The kids who hang out there whisper when we come in. I hear them say, *There goes one crazy motherfucker,* and it's hard to tell whether they're talking about Dave with his apocalypse eyes, the Musician with his filthy jeans and busted boots, or me with my shaking hands, my slurred speech.

People driving down the Pike stop in front of my house to take pictures of the historical marker, and they cross the yard to look at the well, which Jesse James supposedly dug. I watch and wonder what they would say if they could see inside. Stacks of magazines from the eighties, old food, stuff even the Musician was too scared to touch when he cleaned the place out, a smell of piss hanging on the shades, which I keep drawn tight. Members of the Nashville ladies' garden club come and tend the outside of the house, watering the rosebushes, trimming back the boxwood. Greenup Bird puts his paws on the windowsill and barks his head off at them. But I don't mind all the people. I remind myself that, though I've almost paid off the mortgage, this house doesn't really belong to me. I am no more than a squatter, only passing through. A few years ago, the ladies put a pine log wishing well on top of Jesse James's deep dank well, a hanging basket full of fake flowers, like something out of a miniature golf course. Dave gets some work somewhere south of the city and leaves, promising the Musician that he'll give us a call on his cell if he hears from Jesse. The Musician comes down the road and knocks on the door, looking for clues. Frank's house burned in 1909, but the Musician reasons that maybe he left something at Jesse's place, a hint, a tiny bag of gold. *Think we could get down that well?* he asks. He eyes the living room fireplace suspiciously and runs his finger along the mortar. *Do you really think we'll find it?* I ask him. He straightens up, pushes his hand through his wild long hair. He looks more serious than I've seen him in years. *For future generations. We need to find it,* he says. *What the hell are you talking about?* He looks at me. *I'm going to be a father,* he says, grinning like a sphinx. *I'm forty-nine years old. I've never even dreamed of this.*

At the start of October, Dave returns, unannounced, to sleep on the Musician's floor. In the middle of the night he gets word from Jesse that he hasn't been remembering correctly.

Frank didn't put it up on the ridge, Dave reports to us. *He buried it in one of the fields near his house.* The farm that Frank rented was sprawling, hundreds of acres along the creek. It took him days to plow, even with a team of good mules, even with a half-dozen hired hands. We abandon the ridgeline and come down into the valley. We start out from east to west with no regard for fences, property lines, NO HUNTING OR TRESPASSING signs. We dig wherever Dave or the metal detector tells us to: In farmers' fields, in people's backyards. We dig up shale and limestone filled with crinoid fragments and brachiopods, the fossilized skeletons of creatures who inhabited Brown's Ridge 500 million years ago, when we all would have been standing at the bottom of a shallow salty sea. We scare up a half-clothed teenage couple who spook out of the paw-paw like deer. I find an arrowhead, perfectly fluted. When the white man first came, the Indians would lure him into the woods by imitating animal sounds: at night, a fox or an owl; during the day, a squirrel, horse bells. Kaspar Brown was stalking what he believed to be a rutting buck the day that he was ambushed on the steepest part of the ridge.

Joe Guy stands in the gold light of his back field in late October, shading his eyes with one hand. The cows, some of them descendants of his father's herd, the ones he bought back in 1969, have all been trucked to Alabama. A bobcat that he has watched all its life will spend a few weeks cowering under the construction foreman's trailer until it streaks out of the pasture and into the hills. The sadness I feel when I see the backhoes moving in is much bigger than me. It seems to shadow the land with heavy wings. At the Meat 'n' Three, Lacy leans over the toilet in the back and throws up before her breakfast shift, holding her hair at the nape of her neck. Joe Guy comes in for one last breakfast, trying to fill a creeping emptiness. *At least the house will stay in the family,* he mutters, hunched at the counter over his coffee and eggs. *Joe Jr.'s coming back for it, you know.* When Lacy hears this she pauses, her heart pounding and full of new hope, stooped over the bleach bucket with a dripping rag.

B. J. Woodson and J. D. Howard used to ride their horses down the Pike and across the river on Saturdays, taking the Hyde's River Ferry and kicking up dust. Just across the Cumberland, in a floodplain at the bend of the river, was the racetrack where they used to spend their hours, Frank always anxious to get back to the farm, Jesse always convincing him to stay longer. The flat alluvial deposits of the land, the silt and fine-grained sand, made it an ideal place to run horses. Seventy years later, it made it the obvious spot to build the Cumberland County airport, and when they built the runways they dug up hundreds of horseshoes and coins. When the airport moved out to the interstate in the eighties, the floodplain became the MetroCenter Mall: a movie theater, vast parking lots, elaborate fountains. Since it went bankrupt a few years ago it's been all but abandoned, save for one former shoe store at the back, facing the river, that has been converted to the State Democratic Headquarters: Some interns and a couple of laptops, without even a prayer. You can see it from the top of the ridge, this white elephant, and if you know how to look you can see the palimpsest of the land clearly, the story written on top of story written on top of rubble and bone.

Sometimes I don't know where Dave gets it from. He takes things he hears here and there and cobbles them all together into one unified theory of Armageddon. He pushes his greasy black hair from his face, rolls a joint, takes Isaiah from his pocket. *The earth is utterly broken down,* he reads. *The earth is moved exceedingly. The land shall be utterly emptied, and utterly spoiled. It shall reel to and fro like a drunkard.* If this is true, we ask him, why is he bothering to dig for buried treasure? *If we strike it rich,* he says, *I can buy my girl a Greyhound ticket out from Cali. Get a fuck before the end of the world.* The Musician rolls his eyes behind Dave's back. We have spent long hours debating the existence of this girl. If you spend enough time with Dave, it is hard to keep track of what is true. I do know this: I haven't believed in God since the 1960s. These days I'm not sure what I believe in at all, save the law of the conservation of matter, which means everything is made of what came before: the shrapnel of the big bang runs through my veins, the dinosaurs, the mammoths, the cells of the bones and shit of every man, woman, or cockroach that walked this earth before me.

·   ·   ·

Years ago we held huge parties up at the Musician's cabin. We'd roast a pig, plug in the amps, invite loads of music industry people who would drive up from the city, get trashed out of their skulls, and wake up in the morning next to a stranger on the cabin floor. Back then there was no Minute Mart, and people brought beer and liquor in huge metal coolers, not to mention sheets of acid, coke, all the heroin you could ask for. The Musician slept with second-rate country singers and girls just off the bus from Huntsville or Tuscaloosa who were headed for Music Row. I would lock myself in the bathroom with a producer or two and try to slip free of my mind. When my veins started to fall apart, I shot up between my toes. After the stroke, I realized that the world is much bigger than I'd ever before imagined, and that it will close up seamlessly on my absence, like water over a sinking stone. This is the most important thing I know. Walking with Greenup Bird one morning along the creek, I saw him shove his nose into a tangle of thorns. He pulled it out, looked up at me with a startled face, then opened his mouth, and a tiny sparrow flew out from between his teeth and disappeared into the trees.

November comes, and the woods get gray. The leaves crumple into fists. On his good days, the Musician is talking in ten-year plans, stocks, mutual funds. *When we find the treasure*, he says, *first thing I'm doing is getting a mutual fund*. On his bad days, he leaves the metal detector hanging on a hook near the door and drinks himself to sleep in the cabin. Dave's friend's cousin gave him a quart jar of peach-flavored moonshine, and he passed it on to the Musician. Dave quit drinking when he found religion, and he knows I won't touch the stuff now. The Musician will do anything that's handed to him. The moonshine is colored with Kool-Aid and he wakes up on his couch with pink drool stains like fangs at the corners of his mouth. Late one night, Joe Guy Jr. comes back to Brown's Ridge. He drives down the Pike in a new Ford truck, just like his father's, and brings a tape measure to plan how he will furnish the big house, which is already in a choppy sea of broken ground. Lacy wakes up when she hears the distant sound of the truck's big engine and knows, deep in her blood, that it is him. The Musician, when he hears about Joe Jr.'s return the next morning at the Minute Mart, doesn't yet have any reason to think twice about it.

Frank James loved Brown's Ridge, because he could do an honest day's work here. He could spend ten hours behind the plow and have nothing to hide when he fell exhausted into bed next to his wife. He stopped cussing and joined the church. He befriended the Nashville policemen. *Frank was always the level-headed one,* Dave says. *Jesse tells me that all those years on the road, his brother was really just along for the ride.* Just before he leaves for Florida, we run into Joe Guy at the Minute Mart, buying bread and milk. *I seen you boys out there in the field,* he says, not unkindly. *What are y'all doing out there?* The Musician looks down at the toe of his boot. *Not your worry now, is it?* he snaps, taking a swig from a forty in a brown paper sack. Joe nods. It is not his fault, not really. He's just a tired old man. I think I know how he feels.

Joe Guy isn't long gone by the time phase one of Apple Orchard Acres is up. One day it's just a handful of foundations and the next the first families are moving in from the city, bringing boxes of appliances and purebred dogs. The yards are still open sores of fill dirt and truck ruts. The new families plant spindly dogwood trees next to the broad stumps of the hackberries and tie them to stakes with string. They install aboveground pools along the creek line and put out poison meat for the coyotes. I lock up Greenup Bird at home and go out with a garbage bag to collect as much of it as I can, then burn it in the woodstove. The streets of the development are named after apples, part of the orchard theme. Gala Court, Macintosh Way, Granny Smith Drive. *I didn't know that Joe Guy ever had apple trees here,* the Musician says. He didn't. He had Holsteins, and before that it was a tobacco field, and before that, who knows, a Shawnee hunting camp, a battleground in some long forgotten war. *Well, what do names mean, anyway?* the Musician asks. Quite a lot, I think. They used to tell a story. Fred Profitt built a road up his holler in 1957 and we still call it Fred Profitt Road. When the city came around to put up street signs, Jim Harnell named the road up to his place Schlitz Lane. Hyde's Ferry Road dead-ends at the river, and most people don't think to wonder why, now that the boat and landing are gone. Last year I gave Lacy a dog I found on the Pike, a big scary boxer that she feels safer coming home to. She gave me directions to her house so I could drop him off, up on Bear Hollow Road, where in 1873 a man named Zeb Mansker shot and killed a black bear, then covered its hide in salt and left it in his pasture for his cows to lick and rasp clean of flesh. *It's the third house on the left,* she told me. *If you don't count the trailers.*

No one in Brown's Ridge, as far as I know, remembers the girl for whom Katy Creek is named, but I like to think of her, a plain, dark-eyed girl with a temper, and secrets. Downstream, where the water widens before emptying into the big brown Cumberland, there's a one-lane bridge over a stretch that's deep enough to swim in. In the summer the kids jump off the bridge, hollering and whistling. They all know it's okay to jump off the west side of the bridge, but not the east. Rumor has it there's a Pinto rusting underwater just to the east, and you could slice your foot off, or impale yourself, or worse. It's wisdom that's been passed down through years among the kids: *Not there,* they tell the younger ones. *There's a Pinto down there, not there. That's where the Pinto is, the Pinto, the Pinto.* The kids at this point probably have no idea that a Pinto's a kind of car, but then again, the kid who drove it off the bridge twenty-five years ago probably had no idea that a pinto's a kind of horse.

.   .   .

In December two things happen: Brown's Ridge Baptist paves a brand-new parking area, and Lacy's baby starts to show. Every Sunday, more and more people file through the doors of the church in search of salvation. Preacher Jubal rubs his hands together and says, *You are all welcome,* then looks around and pauses, troubled, struck by the fact that he's never seen a black face in the congregation before. After the service he walks to the Meat 'n' Three and orders coffee and a slice of pecan pie. *Why don't I see a nice girl like you in church?* he asks Lacy. Then to no one in particular, *She'll make a good mother. Even to a bastard child.* Joe Guy Jr. eats supper there every night. He eats with his eyes on Lacy, measuring her the way he is measuring the new furniture he will buy for his father's house. She hums and checks to see if the soup in the Crock Pot is hot with her thumb. When she was sixteen, Joe Jr. took Lacy up to one of the shacks on the ridge side and laid her down on the yellowed newspaper and broken glass. In that moment on the ridge, Lacy gritted her teeth and saw clearly what her life was meant to be. Joe Jr. will live in his father's old house, strange among the new brick mansions, and drive every day to Nashville to his job at a used car lot. For the past two years, in the dark of her bedroom at night, Lacy has silently moved her lips and wished for his return, the closest she has ever come to praying.

Dave reads from Isaiah as we hike past the new houses, heading to the edge of the creek. *The streams shall be turned into pitch, and the dust into brimstone, and the land shall become burning pitch. For it is the day of the Lord's vengeance.* The Musician turns around and says, *Oh, shut up. I've got more important things to worry about.* When we pass, the dogs in the new yards throw themselves against the ends of their chains. The houses are enormous, windows piled on windows, pink brick. Every single family that has moved into Apple Orchard Acres has been black, a fact that neither Joe Guy nor any of the developers could have predicted. *Haven't those people been fighting all these years to get out of the country?* Jubal Cain asked the crowd at the Meat 'n' Three. *Why do they want to come back?* The Musician can't get any work laying tile, even in the new houses. The detail work has all been subcontracted out to Mexicans who come up from Nolensville Pike in the backs of crowded pickups. *Look right here,* Dave says, jabbing at the pages of Isaiah. *Strangers shall stand and feed your flocks, and the sons of the alien shall be your plowmen and your vine-keepers. It's all in here,* he says. He shakes the Musician's arm. *Are you sure you should take that all so literally?* the Musician asks him. He's been talking about playing music again, going back out on the road, calling some old friends. Anything to make a little money. He hasn't had work for weeks and we are all living on dried beans and peanut butter. But no new band is going to hire a fifty-year-old bass player, even if he has played with Clint Black and George Strait.

The black families keep coming, moving out from Jefferson Street and Charlotte Avenue. They want a half-acre yard, a three-car garage, no more screaming neighbors. The first night they spend in their new houses, the smell of fresh paint curling their noses, they hold each other and vow to lose twenty pounds, to argue less. Preacher Jubal sits in the Meat 'n' Three and says to the four or five white men eating there, *Now wait a minute, brothers, is this how we want our town to grow?* Lacy gets so big that she can't bend over to wipe the tables, so she leans over and wipes them behind her back. She sits down with us, blows her bangs up from her forehead. *You boys been up to much?* she asks. In her face it's plain that she's quit expecting anything from the Musician. *Not much,* he says, eyes on her belly, grinning. When he finds the treasure, he's going to come for her at work and take her in his arms, tell her he can give her and the baby anything they need. Until then, he's not letting on to anything. He wants it to be a surprise. While we drink coffee, the Musician leafs through a *Pennysaver,* and among the ads for grave plots and truck caps he finds one for a new metal detector, STATE OF THE ART, LCD DISPLAY, $500, OBO. *No,* I say. *Yes!* he says, slapping his hand down on the table. Surveyors' stakes go up in the field across from my house. We find orange tape around the hackberry trees, which can mean only one thing. *Good God,* the Musician says. *It's all going.* He takes off his hat and rakes back his hair. *They're coming out here for the same reason we did, aren't they?* I nod my head yes. *For peace.*

Dave disappears for three days, then comes up to the cabin to tell us we are close. He had a dream that told him so. *It's right under our noses,* he says. All day long, the Musician has been calling friends looking for loans, and he's flat out on the couch, exhausted, his eyes bloodshot and glazed. *Really?* he says halfheartedly, but still feels moved to sit up and crack a beer. Greenup Bird lies in the corner with his head on his paws and follows us with his eyes. *My girl's comin' out,* Dave says. *I talked to her last night. She says the end may come sooner than we think.* He puffs a joint, examines the glowing tip, hands it to the Musician. *I think it's gonna come on real slow,* he says. *Then hit like an atom bomb.* He smacks his hands together. Lacy parks behind the Minute Mart with Joe Jr., who is making wild promises with his hand between her legs. *But he's not yours,* Lacy tells him, for the hundredth time, but he doesn't care. He looks into her tired eyes and feels not love, but a flutter of anticipation, which for him is close enough to it.

Jesse James liked it well enough here, but he was always anxious to get back to traveling. Frank loved this place, and would have stayed forever. He loved the life of B. J. Woodson, simple, honest, repetitious. *I don't know how he did it, settled down like that after a life on the road,* the Musician says. *I could never do that.* Frank and Jesse and their band, all living in the area under assumed names, met at twilight at the saloon, drinking beer and watching the hills light up with the setting sun. All through the spring, without anyone knowing it, Lacy and the Musician were walking up into the back pastures of Joe Guy's farm, making love on a blanket and afterwards picking seed ticks off one another, laughing. He told her stories of his travels, meeting Johnny Cash and Jerry Garcia, and she listened with her afternoon eyes half-closed and probably wished she knew him back in the day, when he was twenty years younger. On the coldest day of January, the Musician drives past the Meat 'n' Three and sees the big Ford parked outside. He slows and sees the two of them through the steamed plate glass door, Joe Jr. leaning across a table, Lacy's chair pushed back to make room for her enormous belly. Without thinking he cuts the engine and pulls over to watch them, panic knocking around in his chest, his finger-nails gouging deep crescents in the steering wheel.

The next morning I look out my window and the stakes in the field across the Pike are gone, vanished, and the field looks exactly as it did before, exactly as it has for the past few hun-dred years, the sparrows rising and falling over it like breaths, the trees' shadows spreading out around its edges. Greenup Bird and I take a slow walk around the perimeter and hear deer footsteps in the water of the creek. For an hour or so, I think that it may be spared. Then in the late morning I hear a thunderous thud and I look out the window to see an army of earthmovers. The house shakes. Greenup howls and scratches his nails along the wood floors. My coffee shudders in its mug. I take a deep breath and try to be fluid, like the creek. In the evening the Musician comes down, knocks on the door all wild-eyed. *Time's up,* he says. *We got to get in there before they do.* We strap on headlamps and start to dig, not waiting for Dave to show up. We go haphazardly, without even the metal detec-tor, the Musician throwing shovelfuls of soil over his shoulder like a madman. As we dig, Lacy is sitting with Joe Jr. on the wide bench seat of his Ford, eating a bucket of fried chicken.

The grease makes the baby turn somersaults. *Feel,* she says to Joe Jr. and puts his hand on her belly. He looks into her eyes and says, *We'll name him Joe Guy the Third.*

All through the cold night the Musician digs. He is now only casting about, digging a foot here, a few inches there, trying to sniff it out. Greenup Bird whines and follows him, nosing at each hole when he leaves it. *Dig, Greenup, dig!* he shouts. Greenup whines and scrapes at the holes with his claws, tags jingling. I huddle in my jacket and doze on and off. When I wake I know where they are by the white clouds of their breath. The Musician digs until morning, leaving craters behind him, cursing Frank and Jesse James. He drops to his knees alongside Greenup and digs with his hands, his fingernails bloody. Still he finds nothing. His son or daughter, like all babies in the womb, turns its head away from the light when Lacy sits down in the weak January sun to smoke her first cigarette of the day. A possum hit on the side of Brown's Ridge Pike slowly decays, picked at by crows and ants, until it is just a spine like a zipper, nothing more. Dave's girlfriend calls to tell him it's too late, she's not coming, not unless he comes up with the money. The Musician goes to the Meat 'n' Three before they open for breakfast and kneels in front of Lacy, begging her to wait. *Trust me,* he says. *I will give you and this baby everything you need.*

· · ·

We keep digging. There is nothing else for us to do. The houses will go up fast, concrete foundations that are bound to shift in this floodplain soil, some drywall and some fake brick siding, and just like it happened at Joe Guy's, in a month there will be a row of houses where there were none before, lined up along the Pike like pigs at a trough. The creek will continue to flood every spring, and people will wake up to find their backyards full of crawdads and cat-fish. There will be streetlights, turning lanes, stoplights. In time people will want a Chili's. They will want a Sonic, a Jack in the Box, an Auto Zone, a Piggly Wiggly, a Ruby Tuesday's. A McDonald's will go up at the crossroads, and the Meat 'n' Three will close. A bobcat's den will be bull-dozed away for a store that sells hair extensions and curling irons. The coyotes will root through Dumpsters for a few years before they are run off to the north, howling as they go. *Lo,* Dave says, clutching the book of Isaiah. *There will be burning instead of beauty. Ruby Tuesday,* the Musician says, resting on his shovel for a moment, the haze in his mind parting. *Isn't that a song?*

If I squint at the field I can almost picture it all now. If I squint harder, I can see the Indians making a dugout ca-noe down by the creek, burning trees to clear space for their crops, and before that, the dire wolves, the saber-toothed tigers, the ferns and giant trees, before that the vast immu-table sea. *With the Lord stood three angels,* Dave reads, *each with six wings. With two they covered their faces, and with two their feet, and with two they did fly. And they cried to one another, holy, holy, holy, is the Lord, the whole earth is full of his glory,* raising his voice to compete with the growling engines of the bulldozers.

Everything changes. Even in Brown's Ridge. Of course I know. Bill Ryan will sit alone in the saloon and talk revolution too loud, not knowing that Jack Earthman, a Nashville sheriff, is sitting next to him and listening carefully as he eats a boiled egg and drinks a beer. After he is arrested, J. D. Howard and B. J. Woodson will gather up their families and leave in the night, never to return. Jesse will be shot and killed a year later, in Missouri, and Frank will grow old selling tours of their childhood home for a quarter. Lacy will be terrified of motherhood and for months will sit and stare at her child, a boy, not knowing what to do. Jubal Cain's heart will tar over with hate until it kills him, and the bulldozers will move steadily up the steepest ridge side. *It is with a sense of despair,* said Frank James, *that I drive away from our little home and again become a wanderer.* The Musician stays up all night with a bottle cradled against his chest, watching tapes of his old days on tour, keeping the volume muted, so he cannot hear the applause. Greenup Bird will outlive me, and will end up in the Nashville pound, where no one will want to adopt him. After two weeks in a cage he'll be euthanized, his body thrown in the city incinerator, and his ashes will fall on the Cumberland River like snow. The houses go up, they keep going up, and for now we stay one step ahead of them, digging. The Musician still hasn't lost hope. *The time is at hand,* Dave reads from the book of Revelation, leaning his shovel against his hip and rolling a joint for the end of the world. *Fear not, for I am the first and the last, he that lives and he who has died. Which is, and which was, and which is to come.*